The Terminal Diner

a novel by

Mary Pat Hyland

For Therese,
Thanks so much for
helping me launch The
book. Enjoy w/ coffee.
& pie !

Love,
Mary Pat

Also by Mary Pat Hyland

3/17 (2010)

A Sudden Gift of Fate - sequel to The Cyber Miracles (2009)

The Cyber Miracles (2008)

This book is a work of fiction. The names, characters, location and plot are the creation of the author and should not be considered real. Although inspired by real life experiences, the characters in the novel do not exist and any resemblance to persons living or dead is purely coincidental.

First edition

June 2011

Printed in the United States of America

Set in Georgia typeface

Cover design by Jocelyn Bailey

Cover photo by Mary Pat Hyland

Author's website: marypathyland.com

In memory of J.S.

With deepest gratitude to my editors

Elizabeth Herrington, David Craig & Jordan Nicholson;

my family of proofreaders: Anne, Sheila, Kate & Patty;

and my cover artist, Jocelyn Bailey.

* * *

Thanks also to my family, friends

and fellow indie writers for their support.

~ Chapter 1 ~

"Men like pie."

Maria Brady gave her oldest daughter that advice when she was 16 years old and Elaina still recalls the moment. It was a misty September morning and frost-nipped vermillion maple leaves tumbled around them as they waited for the marigold flash of the school bus in the distance. Elaina was thinking about that new boy in her class, a transfer from a high school down South. She wanted to get his attention and was desperate for advice. Of course she was too embarrassed to tell her mother she was interested in him. Instead, Elaina mustered up the courage to casually ask her mother what the opposite sex liked, what attracted them. Maria suspected a young man had caught her daughter's eye. She smiled as the bus pulled up. "Men like pie," she said and then waved goodbye. It was the last time they saw each other.

It didn't take Elaina long to discover the truth—and irony—of her mother's words. Later that day she was suddenly promoted to pie maker at The Terminal Diner, the Brady's upstate New York restaurant. The job had been Maria's until the moment she abandoned Elaina, her younger sister Dee Dee and their father Walt after a trucker from Missoula gave her a lingering, hungry look when she slid a perfect slice of lemon meringue pie in front of him.

If Elaina had spent her teenage years like a normal girl, she'd probably understand more about men, such as how one lusty glance can make you dump everything you hold dear and hitch a ride with a stranger on the first interstate going west. Normal never arrived, and its lack of an appearance meant Elaina never could figure out men or her mother's decision. All she knew for certain was the pie thing. Apple, blueberry, lemon meringue, pecan—my God, a man couldn't end a meal without a slice. Every day there *had* to be pie.

Her days back then were full platters of house chores, herding Dee Dee to eat-shower-dress, baking pies at the diner before she went to school and helping Walt close up by eight. Dee Dee spent evenings finishing homework at the diner's counter while Elaina stirred blueberries into thick batter for the next morning's muffins (a favorite overnight recipe from a church cookbook). By the time they got home, Elaina yawned through her homework while Dee Dee sawed away at the cello. Maria had insisted on paying for pricey cello lessons because she said Dee Dee's music talent shouldn't be wasted. She was "going places." Maria never said anything like that about Elaina. Instead, she taught her how to make pies, just as her mother Helena had done for her.

The secret to a great pie was the crust, Maria said. "The dough has to be cold and you shouldn't handle it too much." Maria shared a tip from her mother: "Your Yia Yia Helena always chilled the shortening in the freezer and used ice water to mix the dough." She took Elaina's hand and helped her flute the edge of the dough by pressing it between the middle finger and forefinger with her thumb. "When it looks beautiful, it tastes delightful," Maria said.

Had Elaina focused on her schoolwork, she might have gone to the community college in Binghamton as her best friend Lisa did. Instead, her low grades and reticence to leave the familiar comfort of her small life saved Walt money— enough to pay for Dee Dee's tuition at that private music college in Boston. Elaina wasn't bitter. To be honest, at that time in her life neither man nor potential careers held sway over her heart. Perhaps if her mother stayed around longer and Elaina had gone to college, she would have acquired the self-confidence to make *any* decision on her own and not just about the future. It could have been as simple as deciding to wear Goth eyeliner or dye her hair fuchsia the way Lisa did. Both things she had pondered for a couple of years. Yet today her eyes remained pale and undefined; no rebellion streaked across her hair.

Walt provided no compass for Elaina in these matters. After Maria fled, he anchored himself at the diner they'd bought from her father, Metro. Walt's sanity was held together by the diner's routine, a bond as tenuous as one made with old, amber-hued cellophane tape. He was just 45, yet felt like he was 60. Walt had few friends who weren't customers and as for women, why would he allow his heart to be abandoned again? He was glad that his work provided Elaina with shelter and a steady job—more than his own parents had given him. Walt buried his own dreams of becoming an architect years ago under greasy towers of corned beef hash scraped across The Terminal Diner's griddle. Elaina would have to uncover other dreams on her own. At her current pace of decision-making though, she'd be with him at the diner 'til he dropped dead over some sunny-side-ups.

By the time she was 26, Elaina could do one thing well: bake damn-fine pie. The diner was down the bend from the Binghamton Regional Airport terminal, and Elaina liked to think that her pies were the first or last taste visitors had of Binghamton. Their whole impression of the city might hinge on the flakiness of a crust, the juiciness of seasonal fruit. This wasn't just a job—this was civic pride.

Elaina's pies were so renowned that some customers dropped in regularly when they knew their favorites were on the menu. The plastic pipe salesman stopped in on Wednesdays for the Boston cream. The Lions Club president moved their monthly lunch meetings to Thursdays because of the peanut butter fluff. That cute young state trooper swung by Saturday mornings. Said he couldn't start his day right without a slice of apple crumb warm from the oven.

She'd been in this routine at the diner for a decade now. The week-long ritual of paring fruit, kneading dough and washing pans in hot, lemony-soaped water dimmed what little beauty remained of Elaina's appearance. Her knuckles were swollen like galls on willow branches, rimmed red like ripe peaches. Years of confinement within the stainless steel diner walls blocked sunlight from warming her face and denied natural shimmer from her hair, which picked up a greenish-yellow cast under the kitchen's fluorescent lights. Her looks didn't matter much. In fact, they rarely crossed Elaina's mind.

That particular Monday morning she got to the diner by 5:30 a.m. and had already rolled out several crusts by the time Walt arrived to cook breakfast. He walked over to an Irish pound note framed above the cash register, kissed his fingers and touched it for good luck. His late brother Patrick brought it back years ago after visiting some cousins in County Cavan. Walt dreamed of going to Ireland one day, but not until there was someone who could run the diner completely in his absence. In other words, that pound note was probably as close as he'd ever get to the Emerald Isle.

"Hey, Pop. Did you notice the parking lot sign is gone again?"

"Probably college kids. They sure get a kick out of hanging up 'Terminal Diner Parking' on their dorm walls. I oughta make some copies to sell at the campus book store."

"Did ya ever think of changing the name?"

"Well, it was called The Terminal Diner when we took it over from your grandfather Metro 20 years ago. Maria and I figured it might affect business if we changed it. Like they say, if it ain't broke...."

"I guess, Pop. Hmmm. Feels like it's gonna rain today," Elaina said as she floured a ball of dough and shoved the heel of her hand into it. She glanced up at the clock and noticed that no one had changed the calendar under it yet. And here it was the tenth of the new month already. It must have been because they were so busy last week with the Labor Day

Weekend crowd and back to school bustle. She wiped the flour off her hands and hooked the new month's page onto the nail: September 2001.

"Mary Jo called in sick today. I'm gonna need your help in the dining room waiting tables with Angie."

"No problem, Pop. I'm ahead on the pies. Muffins are done, too." Elaina slid a couple of blueberry pies into the oven and went to set the tables for breakfast. She looked out the front window and noticed a new sign hanging over the former used car dealership across the road.

"Hey, someone's bought Paul Wallace's shop," she called out to her father. "Now it's American Car Sales & Repair."

"I heard a couple of Middle Eastern fellas bought it. Glad to see that open again. We used to get a lot of customers from Paul."

The aroma of brewed coffee and sizzling bacon filled the diner by the time Angie arrived to work at 6:30 a.m. She smiled warmly at the first customers of the day waiting for her, a retired engineer and his wife who knew Walt from church. He peeked out the order window and waved as Angie handed them each a menu.

Angie was his best hire ever. She was a hard worker, always dependable and pleasant to work with. That pertly bobbed ash blonde hair and brilliant smile of hers didn't fool him. Walt knew she'd had a rough life. Her husband Mario was a rock musician who became addicted to heroin and overdosed several years ago after a gig in a downtown bar. They never had kids, which in a way was a blessing for Angie because she was still struggling to pay off the huge credit card debts he incurred.

"Regular or decaf, hon?" Angie poured the coffee and sprinkled a handful of creamers in front of them. By half past eleven, the tables and booths were buzzing with customers and Elaina had already joined Angie out front rushing around to serve them.

"Why is everyone so hungry today?" Elaina mouthed to Angie as she passed her with a tray full of pie slices.

"You'd think it was their last meal on earth, El."

A young man came in holding an umbrella, pulled at his suit jacket (obviously new), and sat down at the counter. He ordered a turkey club sandwich and cola.

"All dressed up," Elaina smiled as she handed him a straw for his drink. "What's the occasion? You look like you're either heading to or coming from a job interview."

"Actually both," the young man said as he wiped his brow. "Man, it's so humid out."

"So, how'd the first one go?" Elaina asked.

The man shrugged and wiggled his hand.

"Now I'm catching a flight to New York this afternoon. I have an interview with a Wall Street firm at four thirty today. If that goes well, I'm meeting with one of the VPs tomorrow morning at their new office in the World Trade Center."

"Ever been to New York before?"

"Of course. Many times. How about you?"

Elaina grinned shyly. "Naw. Someday...."

"Well, if I get this job, any time you want to come down

and see the city I'll give you a tour."

She blushed and smiled as she leaned forward impulsively and tucked a napkin in his collar. "Don't want ya to spill anything on your interview suit." Elaina bustled around the dining room but kept an eye on the young man. As soon as he looked like he was finished, she went back over.

"Get ya anything else?"

"I'm fine, thanks."

"Not even a piece of pie I baked this morning? You know, for good luck."

"Pie? Um...sure. What do you have?"

"Well forget the blueberry 'cause you don't want stained teeth ruining your interview. The apple came out real good today."

He laughed. "You convinced me. Give me a slice of lucky apple pie."

Elaina skipped back to the kitchen and cut a larger than usual slice for the young man. As she handed it to him there was a flash of lightning outside followed immediately by a thunder crack.

"That sounded close," the young man said as he spun around to look outside. "Hope my plane takes off on time."

A man wearing a neon pink Hawaiian shirt, khaki pants and moccasins dashed toward the diner from his car as rain started to fall with fury. He waved a poster at Elaina.

"Excuse me, miss. I was wondering if I could put up this flyer on the bulletin board by the entrance. It's for an exhibit at my gallery."

Elaina read the flyer and stared at the oil portrait of a man leaning against the mast of a sailboat.

"Did you paint that?"

"Yes, I'm Rhey White. I bought the old drive-in theater down the road recently and converted it into a gallery."

"Oh, yeah, I saw some workers down there and wondered what was going on. Look at this," she said as she turned the poster around to show the young man finishing his piece of pie. "Doesn't it look just like a picture?"

Rhey cringed.

The young man nodded. "Wow. That's really good. Wish I had talent like that."

Rhey made a slight bow with his head. "Why thank you, very much. You should both come by my gallery. The show opens Friday." He looked outside at the still insistent rain and grimaced. "Gotta run. Buh-bye."

When Rhey approached the door, a man in a Navy uniform held it open for him. Rhey thanked him as he ran to the car.

"Did he lose the way to Margaritaville or something?" the sailor asked as he sat at the counter.

Elaina frowned as she handed him the menu. "He happens to be a real good artist."

"Definitely has talent," the young man said as he stood up to pay his bill.

"Yeah? Well he doesn't have any talent for fashion. The glare off that shirt just about burned my retinas," the sailor said, laughing loudly while looking around the diner to see if anyone would join in. "Now this kid knows how to dress. Nice suit. Great tie. Whaddya heading to, an interview?"

"Yep, just leaving for New York."

"Ahhhh, the city. Boy, do I have fond memories of The Big Apple." The sailor leaned toward the young man. "You ought to wear one of these outfits during Fleet Week," he said pointing at his uniform. "You'd be beating away the chicks. I'm talking *real* lookers. Not like what you see around here." He nodded toward Elaina.

"Good looks are easy to find," the young man said. "Being able to find a woman who can bake pie as delicious as"—he leaned in to read her name tag—"Elaina's, is far more appealing, I'd say."

Wow, she couldn't believe a stranger defended her honor like that. She wanted to ask what his name was, but didn't have the nerve.

"Yeah, right. Whatever you say, bud," the sailor snorted as he opened a menu.

"Good luck," Elaina waved as the young man walked out the door and opened his umbrella.

"So you think your pie is pretty good?" the sailor asked, tapping her arm with the menu. "I'll be the judge of that. Give me a piece of apple."

"Sorry, we're fresh out." She lied. This jerk didn't deserve a slice of her best pie.

"Got any other fruit pie?"

"Nope. Blueberry's gone, too. I've got pumpkin, coconut cream or pecan left."

"No fruit pie? Forget it. I don't need dessert. Gotta keep my girlish figure."

Ugh, Elaina thought as she noted his name tag said "Johnson." Customers like this guy were why she preferred to work in the kitchen. As she headed back to that comfort zone, she passed Walt carrying in a box of coffee filters to stack under the counter. He noticed the sailor sitting there.

"How long you been in the service, son?" Walt asked with a smile.

"A few years now. My leave is up. Flying back to Virginia."

"You be sure to take care then."

"Yessir."

That evening as Elaina wiped down the tables, she saw lights were still on in the garage across the street. Boy, those new owners must be hard workers, she thought.

Tuesday morning the first hints of dawn warmed the horizon as Elaina neared the top of Airport Road. At the intersection with Commercial Drive, she passed the boomerang-shaped neon sign for Rhey's Drive-In Gallery on the right. It looked like something from that cartoon *The Jetsons*, which made her laugh. When she got out of her car in the diner's parking lot, she noticed the owners of the new dealership across the street were talking animatedly on cell phones, pacing in front of the garage. Lights glowed from inside. Had they even been shut off from the night before? She could hear the owners' voices but they spoke in a language she couldn't understand.

Elaina put the key in the front lock and heard the birds

singing spiritedly around her. The air was as crisp as a bite into a fresh-picked apple and the sky was a rare hue of deep turquoise. It sounded as if the birds were taunting her to play hooky on this glorious morning. She breathed in deeply, paused as she thought about heeding them for a second, and opened the door.

Yesterday afternoon on her break she had driven up Brooks Road to buy late raspberries and blueberries as well as the first of the Cortland apples at the orchard stand. Elaina couldn't wait to use this beautiful assortment of fresh fruits. Today's pies would be especially delicious. She rolled out the pie crusts and wondered if Mary Jo would show up for work. There was a TV movie Elaina wanted to see tonight, and if she didn't have to do Mary Jo's shift in addition to her own, she'd get home in time.

As she wove the lattice strips across the blueberry and raspberry pies, Walt walked by and noticed that along with the apple pies they formed a red, white and blue theme.

"I like the patriotic look you have going there, daughter." Elaina stood back and laughed.

"You're right. Hadn't noticed."

The daily 6 a.m. Xpress Cargo flight into Broome County flew in lower than usual over the diner. With planes coming and going all day long, Elaina was so used to the roar that she rarely paid them notice. This plane made a different noise, as if there might be engine trouble.

"That didn't sound good," Walt said as he poured water into the coffee pot. Elaina peeked out the dining room window to see if there was any black smoke coming from the direction of the airport. No booms. No smoke. The sky looked even bluer, if that was possible.

"Aww, can't we take the day off, Pop? It's too nice out to be stuck inside working."

"I wish. But I *do* have some good news. Mary Jo called to say she'd be coming in to work, but might be a little late."

"Thank God for that," Elaina said as she flipped around the sign on the front door, "Open Monday-Saturday, 6:30 to 8." Despite her best intentions, Mary Jo hadn't arrived before the first customer of the day.

"Elaina, can you take care of him?" Walt called to her.

A tall man with a braided black ponytail sat in the last booth by the front window and placed the rucksack he was carrying next to him. He wore a beaded belt over his untucked jean shirt and a silver turtle on a chain around his neck. His looks made Elaina think he was an American Indian, and she wondered if he was from the Onondaga Nation up near Syracuse.

When she walked over with a menu and held up the coffee pot, he shook his head.

"Hot water."

"Do you want tea?"

"No. Have my own."

After she returned and filled up his mug, he took a sachet from his rucksack and dunked it in the water.

"I'll have the special."

Mary Jo arrived muttering a string of apologies. There was

something about Merle coming home late from third shift and she had trouble waking up the kids for the school bus. Elaina smiled at her as she thought, boy, what a drama magnet.

While arranging fresh muffins in the display case, Elaina saw a reflection in the mirror behind the counter of the men still talking on cell phones across the street. They went inside the sales office, argued for a few minutes, then turned off the lights, came outside, got in their cars and drove away. That's weird, she thought. Closing the shop already? Wonder what's going on over there?

The man in the booth came over to pay his bill. She handed him his change and he replied "*Nyaweñha*," grabbed some free cinnamon toothpicks by the cash register and walked out the door. Elaina wondered what he said.

Mary Jo was busy taking orders, so Elaina cleaned up the man's booth. She picked up the tea bag off his plate and sniffed it. Smelled like pot, she thought. (Once she'd caught Dee Dee and her high school boyfriend smoking it behind the diner. After she told Walt, Dee Dee never tried that again.)

There was no tip left on the table. Elaina frowned. Then a glimmer from the seat of the booth caught her eye. It was a sculpture made with crumpled aluminum foil of a man riding an airplane. The figure was about the size of a coffee cup.

"Hmm, now that's different. Could've used the tip money, though." She sighed as she tucked the sculpture carefully into her apron pocket and carried his dishes into the kitchen.

About an hour later, a car screeched into the parking lot and the artist from the Drive-In Gallery ran inside, breathless.

"Do you have a TV in here?" Rhey yelled. Elaina pointed at the one bolted to the ceiling above the cash register.

"Put it on. It's crazy! I can't believe they've done this!"

"What's going on?" Walt asked as he ran from the kitchen with his spatula. Elaina grabbed the remote control and turned the TV on. "Who's done what?"

"It's gotta be terrorists! Planes! Hit the World Trade Center!" Rhey said. "I just heard about it on NPR. My TV isn't working, so I...."

"What the...?"

Diners left their seats and gathered near the counter as they watched in horror as flames and smoke spewed from the Twin Towers. The news anchor interrupted a reporter on the scene in Manhattan to say that reports just came in of a third plane hitting the Pentagon. Everyone gasped.

"It's another Pearl Harbor," Walt said.

"Here we go, World War Three," one elderly man said with disgust as he shook his head and sat back in his booth to finish his coffee.

Everyone else in the diner froze in place. The images were too unbelievable for their minds to comprehend. As they stood there with mouths gaping, it got worse. Cameras showed people in the World Trade Center standing on window sills, trying to escape the flames, and then falling to their deaths.

"Ohmigod, my ex...Robbie's there! He works in the South Tower," Rhey said as he clapped his hand over his mouth when he saw a man plummeting from the tower. "I can't look. Oh, dear Lord. What if that was *him*?" He turned away and collapsed into a booth. Elaina sat down across from him.

"Hey, calm down. You don't know what's happened yet. Your ex...um...your friend might be perfectly fine." She took his hand.

"How *can* he be? Look at that. How could he get out alive?" Rhey called Robbie on his cell phone. All he got was a beeping signal or a message saying that all circuits were busy.

Another bulletin came over the TV. A separate jet just crashed in a field in Pennsylvania. "*Please* God, make it stop!" Rhey wailed.

"How close is Shanksville to us?" a customer asked. Then, as if on cue, everyone remembered how close the diner was to the airport and looked toward the windows. Walt sensed their panic rising.

"Listen folks," he said. "Don't worry about paying for your meals. Get home to your loved ones. We'll keep pouring the coffee for free as long as anyone wants to stay."

While most did leave, Elaina brought chairs out from the back room so those who remained could sit and watch the special report.

"I better get home, Walt. They'll probably send the kids home early from school," Mary Jo said as she bit her fingernails. He waved her on with the spatula; she grabbed her purse and ran to her car.

A cry went up across the room. "Oh...oh *noooo!*"

Everyone gasped as the South Tower bloomed into a terrifying cloud of collapsing debris. Rhey covered his eyes with his arms and sobbed. Elaina edged into his booth and draped her arm around him, patting his shoulder. She trembled as tears streamed down her face. Then she closed her eyes and wondered how a morning that started off so peaceful and beautiful could evolve into terror so dark and evil. For some reason, her thoughts drifted to those red, white and blue pies she'd baked this morning.

"Oh. I just thought of something," she said as she backed away from Rhey. "That guy who came in here yesterday. Remember him? You met each other when you brought in the gallery poster. He said he wished he had your talent. He was supposed to have an interview in New York this morning."

"I remember—the cute guy in the brand new gabardine suit. Do you know where his interview was?"

"Wall Street. Wait, his second interview was supposed to be in the World Trade...oh no...." Elaina looked at the counter where the young man sat just yesterday and gasped. Through a cruel coincidence she might be connected to this horrific day. She reached into her apron pocket for a tissue and her hand touched the aluminum foil airplane. It freaked her out. Elaina went into the kitchen to get a box of tissues for everyone and threw the sculpture on the spice shelf above her workspace.

"Here," she said, passing out tissues to the remaining customers.

"They just said the FAA has grounded all planes across the country," Rhey said as he grabbed a fistful of tissues and continued calling Robbie on his cell phone. They looked back at the TV just as the North Tower collapsed. He put his hands over his head as if ducking from debris.

"Oh, Lord! This is *insane!*" Rhey rose from the booth and walked away from the TV toward the back room, pacing around tables as he hit redial on his cell phone, over and over.

The remaining patrons spoke in church-hushed tones about horrors they'd witnessed in their lives. Some mentioned World War II; others recalled bloody battles in Vietnam. One customer told about a gruesome multi-car pileup he witnessed on Route 81 during a snowstorm. This moment, however, was something else. It was way beyond anything they'd ever seen or imagined. Terrorists were attacking multiple American icons in one day. How was it possible?

"It's ringing," Rhey screamed from the other room. Elaina ran to his side just as he heard Robbie's voice. He smiled briefly then his face became solemn. It was Robbie's answering machine. Rhey trembled as he wondered, would that be the last time he heard Robbie's voice?

The diner's phone rang and Walt answered. It was Dee Dee, hysterical.

"They took off from *here*, Pop. I'm so scared. What if there are others meant for us? I want to come home but someone said all the highways into New York have been shut down. I don't know what to do. I couldn't get out of here if I wanted." She sobbed loudly into the phone.

"Calm down, Dee Dee. I think the best thing for you to do is stay put in Boston. This is a national emergency, so nobody's going anywhere. Do you have some friends you can be with tonight?"

"Some of the other music majors live in my apartment

building. I'll see if Joachim is in."

"Good. Hold on Dee Dee, your sister wants to talk with you." Walt handed the phone to Elaina, and then turned and wiped the tears streaming across his face. After Dee Dee heard her sister say hello, she just cried as they attempted to speak to each other. It was too much.

"I love ya, Sis," was about all Elaina could muster.

"You, too."

Walt and Elaina closed the diner just before three o' clock.

"I'll follow you home," Walt said to her.

Outside, a sheriff's cruiser with lights flashing sped up around the bend toward the airport. After a few minutes it headed back down Airport Road and stopped just as Walt was getting into his car.

"Hey, Walt," Sgt. Ben Wilcox called out. "FYI, we've closed off the road up ahead by the airport. You can't head up that way."

"Thanks. We were just going home anyway."

There wasn't much traffic. It was as if they were in a "Twilight Zone" episode, Elaina thought, one in which the entire population of a town vanishes on a beautiful, sunny day. Once home, the eeriness continued. Terror was the only "show" on TV. They stared at the set as Walt cooked hot dogs and beans. He opened a bottle of Jameson Irish whiskey and poured them both a tall glass.

"Are we gonna open up tomorrow, Pop?" Elaina winced as she sipped the strong liquor that burned her tongue.

"I've been debating that, Elaina. We might not do enough

business to be worth it, especially with the airport closed. Then again, people might need a place to gather to talk about it all, like they did today. They'll need something comforting—something like a piece of your wonderful pie."

Elaina hugged a throw pillow as she thought back to that morning, before the chaos, and the simple moment when they were admiring her beautiful pies lined up on the counter. "Well...since the pies are already baked, guess I won't need to get to work early. I'll just ride in with you tomorrow, if you don't mind." Walt came over and put his arm around Elaina. For the second time today he started to cry. It was more than she'd seen him cry in his entire life. He'd never shed a tear in front of them after Maria left.

"It's OK, Pop. We'll get through this." She patted his back awkwardly.

"I just don't understand this crazy, upside-down world today. It's like you can't trust people anymore. Why do people have to hurt each other?"

Right then Elaina knew that his tears were not just flowing for the lives lost in New York, Washington and Pennsylvania. She knew Walt was mourning the former life he'd lost when Maria headed west.

That night when she finally calmed down and fell asleep, Elaina dreamed that she was trapped in one of the Twin Towers. A hand came through the smoke and grabbed hers, pulling her out into the daylight. She could hear the birds singing like they did that morning, and a cool breeze brushed her brow as she stared into the deep blue of sky above. The man released her hand and went back inside the burning tower. She never saw his face, heard his voice or had the chance to thank him.

~ Chapter 2 ~

"THOUSANDS DIE IN DAY OF TERROR"

Elaina stared for a few moments at the next day's headline in the local newspaper and the smoking skeletons of the World Trade Center pictured beneath it. It took her breath away. This evil, as President Bush called it, shattered even the mundane peace of her little life. She skimmed through all the stories to see if there was any mention of that young man who'd stopped at the diner Monday. Her search was futile. Perhaps it was too soon to hear anything, though. The morning TV shows were full of people holding up photos of missing loved ones or tales of others escaping the collapsing towers by unbelievable chance. The dust, literally, hadn't settled in New York.

Mary Jo called to say she might not make it into work. Walt assured her that business would be slow, so she probably wouldn't be needed. "We'll give you a call should things really pick up, but I doubt it," he said. "I don't know what to expect today."

Elaina was so used to planes flying overhead that she barely noticed their approach to the airport. Today it surprised her to see how quickly she noticed their absence. On that clear morning, as she drove to work with her father, it was very odd to look up and see no contrails in the sky. How she yearned for a low roar coming from the west to signal that yesterday was just a horrific dream. Usually they didn't turn on the TV set until it was cleanup time at the diner. This morning it was the first thing Walt did after tapping the pound note hung by the cash register.

Walt tried to decide what the special should be for the day. He'd have to make something that would keep well if there were no customers. It would be important to cook something that people would find comforting, too. Elaina found him staring at the contents of the cooler.

"Meat loaf. Mashed potatoes with gravy. Side of green beans," she suggested as she walked out to the front door to flip over the OPEN sign. Elaina noticed that the car dealership across the street was still dark. Was it closed for good or just out of respect for what occurred? A thought flickered when she remembered the owners were Middle Eastern that there could be something more sinister going on across the road. It'd be the perfect spot for terrorists—within walking distance of the airport. Should anything be mentioned to the police about the strange activity over there yesterday morning? Or was she just being paranoid? She rubbed the chill away from her arms and went back to work.

The first customer walked in around 10 a.m. He sat at the counter, ordered a cup of black coffee and watched the news coverage in silence. A few more straggled in around noon and joined him at the counter. One woman ordered a bowl of soup. Most had just coffee. They were all too distracted to eat, it seemed.

Elaina looked at the beautiful pies she'd made yesterday.

No need for them to go to waste. She cut up a few slices of each and brought them around to customers.

"We have free pie today," she said encouraging the customers to help themselves. Quietly they each took a slice and ate with their eyes focused on the TV, not on the work of culinary art before them—fruits picked at their peak of flavor and the feather-light pie crust that was Elaina's signature. It didn't matter to her. She was just glad to see them being eaten, and happy that they could give their customers comfort.

By mid-afternoon, the clientele dropped off sharply. Walt was just about to call it a day when Rhey pulled into the parking lot. He had horrible bags under his eyes and looked so frail to Elaina. She hadn't noticed before how thin he was.

"You OK?"

He gave her a hug and sat down at the counter.

"Haven't heard a *word* from Robbie yet. Can't get a hold of his partner, Paulo, either. I don't know what to do. You can't go into New York this morning. I left another message on his answering machine, but what if it's never heard?" He put his head down on the counter and wept. Elaina handed him a tissue as Walt poured him a cup of coffee. Rhey sat up, put his elbows on the counter and wrapped his hands around the mug. As he sipped, Elaina slid a slice of raspberry pie next to him.

"You better eat something to keep your strength up, Rhey." Walt said. "No charge today for pie or your coffee."

Rhey mouthed "Thanks." He tried to pick up the fork but his hand was shaking. Elaina reached over and steadied it so he could get the pie into his mouth. She rubbed his back gently as he ate. Rhey finished the slice quickly.

"Guess I was hungrier than I thought."

"How about a sandwich, son? Or a hot dog?"

"Or meat loaf with mashed potatoes?" Elaina interrupted. Rhey nodded and Walt went back into the kitchen. "Pop, get him a cup of soup, too."

An ambulance pulled up. A group of EMS workers came inside and sat at the first booth. Elaina went over to greet them.

"Hi, we're here for a quick bite before we hit the road," one said. "Headin' down to New York to help out at the World Trade Center. They're overwhelmed."

"We have a meat loaf special today. No charge. How does that sound?"

"Really? That's great!" they all said. "Thank you."

Rhey overheard them talking and pulled a photo out of his wallet.

"Excuse me, but this is my friend Robbie. He works in the South Tower. If any of you see him down there, would you tell him to call Rhey in Binghamton?"

The squad members looked at each other grimly. One took the photo, examined it carefully, and handed it back to Rhey.

"You can count on it." He nodded.

Before the EMS crew left, Elaina handed them a bag containing the boxed-up remaining pies, napkins and plastic forks and knives. Someone who needed it most would eat those perfect pies.

"You gonna be OK, son?" Walt said to Rhey as they all

walked out to the parking lot.

"I think so. Thank you both for your kindness. Don't know how I could have gotten through today and yesterday without it."

Walt and Elaina ate meat loaf for dinner that night as they stared at the TV again all evening. It was heartbreaking to see the cameras pan telephone poles and bulletin boards papered with flyers seeking news on missing loved ones. When they showed live shots of the rescue workers climbing over that terrible nest of steel and debris, despite the fires still raging underneath, Elaina shook her head. Could anyone possibly be alive under that? Could this ever be cleaned up?

That night she had the dream again. Only this time she noticed that the person pulling her from the fire had a blue shirt on. Was it a cop? A fireman? An EMS worker?

On their way to work Thursday morning, Walt and Elaina noticed American flags flying from many homes along the route even though it was before dawn. Had they been put up after the attacks, she wondered, or were they there all along, just part of the scenery? The road to the airport above the diner was still blocked. The business across the street, still closed. The gray sky above, still empty.

Today some of the regular patrons showed up for breakfast. The Lions Club hadn't canceled so she had to make sure there was peanut butter fluff pie for their lunch. All the while she worked out back, the TV was on in the dining room. Patrons glanced up at it from their meals occasionally. Mary Jo had to leave early for a dentist appointment, so Elaina waited tables in the afternoon for her.

While pouring coffee and handing out straws for sodas, she tried to listen to all the conversations coming from every booth. It seemed everyone had a story. One woman's brother was a fireman in Brooklyn who went down to Ground Zero, as it was being called now, to help with rescue and recovery. Another woman said that Muslims all around the U.S. had been shooting off their guns in celebration. There were gunshots heard an hour down Route 17 from Binghamton in Delaware County, she said. A man who overheard the conversation said they'd been heard up here by the airport, too. Elaina glanced out the window at the business across the road. The office and garage were still closed. Were they training future terrorists at night across the street?

"I was watching the TV and they interviewed this man who was trapped in a stairwell. It was pitch black, filled with smoke. The man got down on his knees so he could breathe better when suddenly another man grabbed his hand and pulled him outside into the light. He said the guy who rescued him had the bluest eyes he'd ever seen, so blue that in the utter chaos of the moment he noticed and remembered them."

Elaina froze with the coffee pot. That sounded exactly like her dream.

"Well you know what the blue eyes mean," another woman said. "That man was an angel. I once heard that psychic Jeremy Candor say that if a stranger helps you do something very special or rescues you, and he has blue eyes, it's really an angel."

Was there an angel in a blue shirt trying to rescue Elaina from something?

Rhey walked in looking more exhausted than yesterday.

"I called the hotline for Robbie's company. They said no one on his floor or above it had made it out. A friend told me about a list online of patients who'd been admitted to hospitals in Manhattan. His name isn't on it. Oh, Elaina...I think this means he really is...."

Elaina hugged him before he finished. Some customers got out of their booths and came over.

"He OK?" one said.

"His friend is among the missing," Elaina said quietly. One by one, each customer came over to give condolences to Rhey. The women hugged him. Men shook his hand or patted his shoulder. It was as if a wake for Robbie was taking place in the diner.

"What should I do about my gallery opening?" Rhey asked Elaina later. "Who will want to go out tomorrow night?"

"Maybe you should hold a vigil for the victims there," Walt said.

"We could light candles in honor of your friend—even that guy who came in here Monday," Elaina added.

"I'd go to it," Angie said. "I feel helpless, like there's something I should be doing but I don't know what."

A local TV news crew entered the diner, approached Walt and explained they'd just been up at the airport filming a story about new security measures. The reporter asked Walt if he knew that the road right under the far end of the runway had been closed for security reasons.

"Would you mind if we interviewed some of your customers? We're trying to get community reactions to these security measures, maybe see if someone here knew someone affected by the attacks."

"Ask and ye shall receive," Angie whispered to Rhey as she picked up the decaf pot.

Walt brought the reporter over to meet Rhey.

"I have no problem with it as long as the customers don't mind. You might want to start with this fella. He's missing a buddy."

Rhey told the reporter how he was changing his gallery opening tomorrow, just down the road, into a vigil for Robbie. He invited any families who are missing relatives, friends or loved ones to join them at 7 p.m.

"Thank you, we'll put this on tonight's news," the reporter said to Rhey when the camera was turned off. "Hope you get a good turnout."

Elaina asked Walt if she could get off work by six Friday to help Rhey prepare for the vigil.

"Sure. I'll probably just close early and put up a sign directing people down the road to the gallery. Check the storage closet before you go. I think there might be a box of votive candles in there left over from the Lions' Christmas party."

After work, Elaina stopped at the grocery to buy ingredients for baking chocolate chip cookies to serve at Rhey's vigil tomorrow. There might be children attending it, and she thought the cookies would give them some comfort in these frightening times. She saw clear plastic hors d'oeuvre plates were on sale and put two sets in her shopping cart along with the matching cups. She wondered if Rhey planned to serve any beverages. He'd need something non-alcoholic if families were there. What about that punch her mother made for Dee Dee's birthday party when she turned ten? She steered herself toward the juice aisle and tried to remember the combination of flavors that had tasted so good that hot August day. Elaina picked up a pineapple juice can and a jug of cranberry. Were these the flavors? She set them back on the shelf, undecided if they were right. Did she add ginger ale or was it a lemon/lime soda? What was the proportion of soda to juices? Why couldn't she remember?

Her mind was distracted from recalling her mother's recipe by a song playing over the grocery's sound system. It was Israel Kamakawiwo'ole singing "Somewhere Over The Rainbow" as he strummed a ukulele. His plaintive voice had the quality of a mother singing a lullaby. Tears rushed down her face instantly like waters through a breached dike. She couldn't hold them back. There in Aisle 3, Elaina bent over her shopping cart and sobbed. Oh how her heart ached, not just for the dead but for herself.

She wished there was a man in her life now, someone who could wrap his strong arms around her and tell her the world would be OK again. But how could she meet anyone, stuck at the diner all those long hours? The few chances she had to go were with Lisa on weekends. They'd go hear her boyfriend

Lenny's death metal band—The Rabid Carousel Horses—play at Cubby's Joint in downtown Johnson City. Metalheads and their tribal piercings gave Elaina the creeps, as if they were just a few brain cells ahead of zombies. Lisa spent most of her time flirting with freaky-looking guys as they crowded around her. Elaina, always the designated driver, stood outside the crush, feeling invisible as she sipped a cola. She'd never meet a guy hanging out at Cubby's, that's a given. If only her mother hadn't left before she grew up. Maybe she'd have instructed her on something more useful than pie making—how to meet decent guys.

The rush of sad memories made Elaina sob harder. She thought of Robbie and the nameless young man who stopped at the diner that day. Both dead, probably. No one paid any attention as she cried for several minutes. Other shoppers in the store just shuffled past, their eyes glazed.

Elaina drove herself to work Friday morning. There had been an increased demand for apple pie, probably a gut patriotic response to the attacks, and that's all she planned to bake today. At least three cars she passed on Airport Road had American flags flapping from their antennas. Trends sure start fast, she thought.

That day, diners watched President Bush tour Ground Zero and praise the workers, vowing to get the terrorists who perpetrated this heinous crime.

"He's gonna get the job done," one man said. "I can feel it. We'll bomb them al-Qaidas so fast they won't know what hit them." The minute the man finished those words, the first arriving flight since the air traffic ban was lifted roared overhead. There was a flash of dread on the customers' faces that faded quickly as they realized it wasn't going to crash into anything. It was a good sign that the worst was probably over for now.

"I'll never trust the sound of a low-flying plane again," one woman said as Angie handed her a grilled cheese sandwich and fries.

Rhey's gallery was in the former drive-in theater's building. He'd had the outdoor movie screen repainted—the theater had been idle for several years—and converted the building holding the projection booth and snack shop into a small gallery space with an attached apartment. Someday, when the business took off and he could invest in fixing up the car speakers and sound equipment, he hoped to show art films there regularly. Until then, he thought it would be fun to have themed slideshows of works currently in the gallery once a week. He'd rigged up a computer to the projector recently and tested it out one night on the big screen. It worked quite well. He was busy looking at images of candles when Elaina arrived with supplies for that night.

"Come in, El. I'm just setting things up."

Elaina was surprised to see a modern interior inside such a retro-looking building. New hardwood floors replaced the worn flecked linoleum. Track lighting set a comforting mood. Rhey's oil portraits were hung around the room. In the center was a painting on an easel, a portrait of Robbie that Rhey finished quickly the night before.

"Wow, Rhey. It looks just like his photograph." She moved in to get a closer look and caught a strong whiff of gum turpentine from the canvas.

"Don't get too close, El. The oils are still wet. I figured we could set out votive candles on the floor around it so no one gets too close."

"It's just beautiful," she said as she took his hands. "What a good-looking guy."

Rhey sighed and nodded. "He was the love of my life. We met at the Rauschenberg retrospective at the Guggenheim. Robbie had an MBA from Wharton; I had a Masters from NYU in arts administration. We opened a gallery together in a snug little Soho space. It was a storybook romance, until Paulo, this eco-printmaker from Brazil showed up to write a new chapter. Robbie arranged for his debut New York show and within a month fell out of love with me and into...well, no need to bother you with the gory details. I was devastated and my Aunt Tillie convinced me to move back to the area. Art can bloom anywhere, she told me. She's been my de facto parent ever since my mother Judyth died." Rhey grabbed a tissue and wiped his eyes. Elaina didn't know whether to hug him or let him cry. Finally she spoke.

"I baked some chocolate chip cookies for kids if they stop by. In this bag are plates and cups. I'm going to try to recreate this punch my mother used to make."

"Aww, you're so thoughtful. Let's take them into the kitchen." He led her through the door that connected to his apartment. It was a simply appointed bachelor's pad with a small kitchen, bathroom, living room and bedroom. Every wall was covered with framed original art.

"Did you hear the president today?" Rhey said as he opened the box of cups. "Wonder how long it will be before we're at war?" They looked at each other, both thinking about what changes in their lives were ahead. He grabbed a bowl from a cupboard shelf for the punch and Elaina stirred the juices and soda together in it with a ladle and added ice. "Let's put the refreshments on a card table along the back wall. There's a linen tablecloth in the drawer next to you. By the way, I have a photo of a candle that I plan to project on the movie screen tonight, once it's dark. I haven't decided, but I was thinking of maybe showing it every night at 9:11 p.m. Maybe leave it on for a half hour or so. What do you think? Is that overboard?"

"No, it's a really nice idea. Imagine people flying in on a plane seeing it. Or the people who can look out their windows toward the hilltop and see it. It will be a touching tribute."

"Don't let me forget to put out the guest book for everyone to sign tonight. I think I'll put it on a table to the right of Robbie's portrait."

One of the first to arrive that evening was the reporter from the TV station and his cameraman. He confided to Rhey that his cousin was missing too. He worked for an insurance company in the North Tower. It had been quite difficult for the reporter to cover the story once he found out. Rhey hugged him and thanked him for coming, then asked if he'd mind being the first to sign the guest book.

By the time the vigil started at seven o'clock, there were about thirty people gathered in the gallery. Rhey lit the votive candles around Robbie's portrait and dimmed the lights. Walt and Angie were there. So were Mary Jo and her husband Merle and four kids. They stood in silence, as Rhey read off Robbie's name and those of other victims connected to the Binghamton area. He finished with "and the young man who left our airport on September 10th for an interview on Wall Street the next day. Though he's nameless to us all, we shall never forget him."

Rhey invited anyone who felt empowered to speak to step forth and do so. One man cleared his throat and recited a poem he'd gotten in a mass e-mail dedicated to "The Brothers": firefighters, police and emergency responders who lost their lives that day. A teenage girl recited lyrics to her uncle's favorite Bruce Springsteen song, "The Brokenhearted." Her uncle, a transit worker, was thought to have been killed as he evacuated people from the subway underneath Ground Zero. After an awkward pause with no one else speaking, Walt stepped forward and choked out a somber rendition of "God Bless America." Slowly, everyone linked arms and sang in a circle around Robbie's portrait.

"Thank you all for coming tonight to celebrate Robbie's life and all the others we've lost," Rhey said. "The gallery is open as long as you want to stay and talk. Art can be a soothing distraction in times of distress. If you'd like to sit in silence and look at the works, be my guest. I'm glad my little gallery could be a peaceful place for all of us to gather this night. Please sign the guest book before you leave."

A few people lingered until Rhey flicked on the projector and a giant candle glowed from the top of Mt. Ettrick. Then they drove off solemnly into the night.

~ Chapter 3 ~

It was life during wartime.

A month later, not only were U.S. troops battling terrorists burrowed in the mountains of Afghanistan, but domestic security was under attack from an unknown foe.

"Great. I'm just getting used to low-flying planes again and now I have to worry about anthrax in the mail? Sweet fancy Moses! Am I not paranoid enough?" Rhey shook his head as he put down the newspaper to stir his coffee.

"My cousin leases a place at the Jersey Shore," the man next to him at the counter said. "After he opened his rent bill that was postmarked Trenton, he started having trouble with his arm and now his doc has him taking Cipro."

"Ohmigod, was it anthrax?" Elaina asked.

"Why else would he be taking Cipro?" the man said. "You won't read about *that* in the papers."

"Or this," the man next to him said. "I heard that plane in Shanksville wasn't heading for the Capitol or the White House. It was heading for Three Mile Island. They were going to make it into a *nuclear* attack."

"Thanks for sharing those cheery tidbits, gentlemen. Oy, I'm definitely not going to sleep tonight." Rhey put his hands over his ears.

"I think there's a lot going on out there that the

government *and* the media don't want to tell us because it would scare the bejesus out of us," the man next to him said. They nodded in agreement.

Elaina stepped behind the counter to set the coffee pot down. As she looked up, she could see in the mirror on the wall that American Car Sales & Repair had finally reopened across the street.

"Hey, is it me or does anyone else think it's weird that the Arabs running the place across the street call it 'American'?" a customer asked Rhey. "You know, 'cause they're Arabs and the first plane to hit the Twin Towers was an American airliner."

"Oh great. Are you suggesting I also have to fear jihad in my neighborhood?" Rhey grimaced. "I better get back to the art bunker and check my peanut butter supplies." Rhey paid his bill, stood up and air-kissed Elaina goodbye.

As she watched him walk toward his car she noticed that every single vehicle in the parking lot had an American flag on its antenna. Elaina thought about mentioning to the men at the counter what she witnessed the morning of 9/11, when the new owners of the business across the street were yelling into their cell phones. When the words began to form in her mouth, though, she saw the mechanic come out of the garage and run across the road toward the diner. Yikes! Can they read my mind?

"Excuse me miss, do you have a bandage? I just cut myself and don't have anything to put on it."

Elaina had never met a Middle Easterner before. She looked at her father who was watching closely from the order window. He nodded at her.

"Sure," she said handing him some napkins to stem the bleeding. "Have a seat and I'll get you one."

While she headed toward the kitchen, a man sitting in a booth waved her over and whispered, "Be careful. This might be how they spread anthrax in here." She looked back at the young man who seemed in genuine pain and frowned at the man at the counter.

"I don't think so."

The mechanic's wound wasn't too deep but bled quite a bit. Elaina wiped his hand carefully with a soapy cloth, put antibacterial spray on it, dried it off and applied a large bandage. A hush fell over the diner as the customers watched in disapproval.

"Thank you very much. I will repay you for this," he said.

"Don't worry about it," she said looking at the faces watching her. "You just be careful." He nodded gratefully to her and ran back across the road.

Another customer at the counter stood up even though his meal wasn't finished. He threw his money on the counter and said, "Hope I don't need Cipro to dine here anymore." As he passed Elaina he wagged a finger at her. "You better be careful who you keep company with, girlie."

She was keeping company with Rhey a lot these days. He was probably ten years older than her, and far more sophisticated, but somehow they forged a friendship quite easily. Rhey was everything Elaina wished she could find in a man. Funny. Kind. Good looking. He even gave her great advice on best shopping buys at the mall, too. Just her luck he wasn't straight.

So what if this relationship couldn't be more? His unique, artistic outlook on everything made life fun. He was much more interesting than her old friend Lisa, who was stalled in mondo metalhead mode. Rhey was a walking encyclopedia of home décor. Elaina had never, *ever* met anyone who had a collection of napkin rings in various shapes and textures for every occasion. For all his elegance, Rhey had a silly side, too, that she just loved. Whenever they'd go to the mall, they'd have to stop at that gag gift store so he could wind up shelves of walking teeth and watch them rattle on. Sometimes they'd drop by the edgy clothing shop where Lisa worked. Rhey was always very polite to Lisa. Her response, Elaina noted, was to act like a snot and glower at him. He never said a bad word about Elaina's friend, but she could tell by her body language that Lisa thought he was weird.

There was such a difference in the two friendships. When Elaina hung out with Lisa, the conversation always morphed into the latest installment of her "soap opera" relationship with Lenny. When Elaina hung out with Rhey, they discussed art, music, travel—life in general outside of Broome County. He'd leave her feeling uplifted, as if there truly could be different possibilities for her life besides making pies. After she spent a few hours in his gallery, Elaina would often sketch pictures inspired by the art she saw on the diner's grocery list. Doodles soon crowded out produce on the list.

Rhey kept encouraging her to take risks. The Italian

burgundy nail polish she bought at the department store makeup counter was his idea. As was his coaching on how to wear a scarf like Grace Kelly. "Drape it over your head, crisscross the corners in front and tie it behind the neck," he instructed.

She was wearing a black and white hound's-tooth check scarf tied perfectly in Grace Kelly fashion that wintry morning the following March when her car slid off Airport Road into a culvert. Her father was already at work, and she was arriving late because of a dentist appointment. It was useless to wait for him to pass by again. She wished she carried a cell phone like Rhey. It would have helped right now. A county sander truck drove past but didn't stop to help. At least he saw her, Elaina thought. Maybe he'll radio in to the sheriff's department.

A pickup climbed the hill slowly and Elaina thought it might stop, but it kept on track and disappeared around the bend. Shortly after, a tow truck going downhill slowed, made a U-turn and pulled up alongside. The side of the truck said American Car Sales & Repair. It was the mechanic she'd bandaged a while back. He signaled to Elaina to get out of the car and into his truck. A flash of fear overcame her and she froze in her seat. He rolled down his window.

"Come, I will drive you to work, then return and get your car. OK?"

She didn't know what to do. At least if she disappeared, that sander truck driver saw her and maybe the sheriff would pass them along the way. She opened the car door and walked carefully over to the tow truck.

"Thank you," she said. "It was kind of you to stop."

"There are many accidents this morning. I've been very busy already."

"I bet. They usually do a great job keeping this road to the airport clear. I think the temperature dropped suddenly after the snow fell this morning."

"Yes. You are right. Temperature is a tricky thing." He smiled and Elaina got a feeling in her gut that it was safe to get a ride from him. She released her tense posture and sat back into the seat more comfortably.

"By the way, I'm Elaina. What's your name?"

"I am Zahir. It is nice to meet you."

"So...where are you from, Zahir?"

"Queens. We are from Queens."

I meant what country are you from, Elaina thought, but she didn't want to push it.

"Have you been a mechanic long?"

"I've been learning this trade for a while. I am hoping to be admitted to Binghamton University and get a degree in engineering. Right now I take some classes at the community college."

"Good for you. That's great. I bake pies. Do you like pie?"

"Yes. Very much. I like apple pie very much. After all, we are *American.*"

Elaina didn't know whether to take his emphasis as coming from a terrorist trying to keep his cover or if he was making a joke because of the name of his business. So she nodded and smiled. It was the safest response, she thought. He pulled the tow truck into the diner's parking lot, jumped out and opened the door for Elaina. As she took his arm for support before she stepped down, she noticed that he had blue eyes.

"I'll tow your car to the shop first and make sure it is OK."

"Thanks, Zahir," she said slowly, distracted by his eyes. "And I'll be sure to have an apple pie baked by then."

He grinned. "I'll look forward to that, Elaina."

All eyes were on her when she walked into the diner. Customers whispered as she removed the scarf from her head. "She looks like one of those Muslim women," a man at the counter muttered.

"What happened, Elaina?" Walt said. "You all right?"

"I slid into a ditch on Airport Road. Zahir, the mechanic across the street, is gonna tow my car to his shop and check it out."

Butch Polakovich, a diner regular, waited at the cash register to pay his bill.

"Tell me, Elaina, did your A-rab boyfriend give you that scarf?" he teased. "Didn't think you were the type to consort with terrorists."

"For your information, Butch, he's not my boyfriend *or* a terrorist. He's repaying us for helping him out. *AND, by the way,* he's studying engineering at Broome Community College."

"Engineering what? Suitcase nukes?" Butch guffawed.

"That'll be enough, Butch," Walt said through the order window.

Butch grabbed a cinnamon toothpick from the dish, stuck it in his mouth and mumbled out the door.

As Elaina put on her apron, Angie carried some dirty dishes past her into the kitchen.

"How do you know he's not gonna steal your car or plant a bomb under the hood?"

Elaina glared at her.

"That's not going to happen."

"How do you know?"

"Because, he has blue eyes."

"An A-rab with blue eyes?"

"I know, weird, huh? A customer told me that if a stranger helps you and he has blue eyes, then it could be an angel."

"Let me feel your forehead a sec, hon. Gotta see if you've got a fever or somethin'."

"Go away," Elaina laughed.

Rhey stopped by for a late lunch. He was reading a curtain catalog when Elaina took her break.

"Look at these, El. Wouldn't they just be adorable in your kitchen?"

"C'mon, Rhey. Do you think Walt Brady would allow something that cute in his house?"

"Well, after all, he lets *me* in the door."

Zahir walked in holding out Elaina's car keys.

"Your car is fine. I had to adjust the alignment just a little, but no other damage from the accident."

"Thanks so much. What do I owe you for your work?"

Zahir held up his hand.

"Nothing. You did me a favor before, I repaid it."

"Hold on a second," she said as she ran back to the kitchen.

Rhey looked Zahir up and down and then smiled at him. Part of him wanted to chat up this handsome young man; part of him feared that he could be the jihadist in the 'hood.

"Here, then. As I promised," Elaina handed Zahir a boxed apple pie. "Thank you for being my angel today."

Walt came over and introduced himself, shaking Zahir's hand.

"Thanks for rescuing my daughter this morning. Much obliged. How's business over there?"

"We're building up customers slowly. It's a little bit difficult these days. You understand," he said looking at the customers staring their way. "We hope word of mouth will help."

"Say, my truck's been idling a bit rough lately. Could I leave it with you tomorrow?"

"Sure Mr. Brady. I'd be very happy to take a look at it. Just tell Malik or Arif that we spoke if I'm not there yet."

"By the way, Zahir," Elaina interrupted, "this is my friend Rhey. He owns the art gallery down the road, where the old drive-in was."

"Oh, yes. The candle. I can see it every night from my window at home."

"Nice to meet you, Zahir," Rhey smiled nervously as he thought, uh-oh, this guy could well be a jihadist in the 'hood.

While they were talking, two women walked up to the cash

register to pay their checks.

"I don't know how some people can be consorting with terrorists while our young men are dying in Afghanistan," one said as she gave Angie her money.

"That's right," said the other. "And freedom isn't free!"

Rhey's eyes widened as he saw an uncharacteristic look of anger flash over Elaina's face. She spun around toward the women.

"Um, ladies, this guy's *not* deaf. Don't be so rude! And, by the way he's *not* a terrorist! He's American and his family is from Queens!"

The women snorted at her. "Yeah, and the pope's my father," one muttered as she pushed open the door. "I believe I'll be taking my business elsewhere."

"Fine!" Elaina snapped. "We don't need customers like you!" Her anger brought a slight smile to Zahir's face.

Walt interrupted the heated exchange.

"Ma'am, this young man rescued my daughter this morning after her car slid off the road. I don't think a terrorist would waste his time doing that. Do you? His business is across the street. Look at the name. It's American—not bin Laden—Car Sales & Repair. And that's where I'm taking *my* car tomorrow."

Rhey sniggered while Zahir stared at the floor. The woman huffed and climbed into her van. Elaina noted that her car had not only an American flag attached to the antenna but flag ribbon magnets and a Semper Fi bumper sticker.

"Man, that was some bee in her bonnet," Rhey hissed. He

made Zahir laugh, which was good because he'd felt so uncomfortable during the awful exchange.

Elaina was fuming. Zahir had rescued her this morning from the ditch. He shouldn't be subjected to such hateful comments. What an ignorant old cow, she thought. It must be so tough right now to be an American of Middle Eastern descent. Even more difficult if you were Muslim, too. How awful Zahir must feel to have people always staring at him and assuming he wants to blow up something.

Despite the altruistic thoughts she had at that moment, later that night when Elaina put her car keys in the ignition, she thought about Angie's warning of a bomb being placed under the hood. For a second, she considered popping the hood to take a quick peek. Then she noticed in the rearview mirror that the light was still on in American's garage. What if Zahir was watching and saw she didn't trust him?

Aw hell, she thought, if I die now, I die now. She turned the key and held her breath briefly. There were no pyrotechnics. What she did notice once she drove away was that her car must have been out of alignment before her accident because it steered much easier now.

On Monday it felt as if an early spring had arrived. The day was clear, sunny and the temperature flirted with the high 60s. Although it wasn't pecan pie day, Elaina had baked one as a surprise for Rhey. She was sitting at the counter reading the newspaper when he came in.

"Look at these headlines: 'Enron scandal threatens to tumble world markets,' 'Suitcase nukes a real threat, expert says,' 'Casualties mount in Afghanistan.' I'm just not going to think about bad news today."

"Good attitude there, El," Rhey smiled.

"Hang on! I've got a surprise for you." She disappeared toward the kitchen.

"You've got Rupert Everett wrapped up for me in the back room?" Rhey called out. A woman in a far booth raised her eyebrow. He shrugged at her and laughed.

Elaina returned with her arms behind her back. "Now close your eyes."

"I love surprises," Rhey said obeying her.

"OK, open them."

"Pecan pie! Why you *temptress*." He blew an air kiss to Elaina. "You're too good to me." His cell phone rang and Rhey answered.

"Hello? Paulo! How are you doing? I was thinking about you and Robbie just the other.... They found what? *Oh Lord*...."

Rhey pushed the pie away, covered his eyes and crunched himself into the edge of the counter. He kept nodding, and as he listened, his hand slid down to cover his mouth. Elaina could see he was crying and walked around the counter to his side.

"Yes, thank you so much for letting me know." He turned off his phone and began to cry. "I gotta get some fresh air, El." She followed him out and they sat down at the picnic table on the lawn next to the diner.

"Paulo just got a call. They've identified Robbie's remains."

Elaina clasped her hands over her mouth.

"All they found was his jawbone and bottom teeth. They were able to identify him with dental records." Rhey looked at the sky as a torrent of tears flowed down his face.

"It's just so ironic...you know...because, of course he had this *Adonis* body. But the one thing you... you always noticed... Robbie had this amazing...it was...his...his beautiful smile." Rhey turned toward her, looking as helpless as an abandoned baby. He cried so hard his body shook. Elaina wrapped her arms around him and held on tight. She cooed softly as she stroked his hair.

"I know this is horrible for you, Rhey, but, at least now you know. So many people never got this closure." He nodded and hugged her tighter. "Ohhh, my beautiful Robbie," Rhey sobbed.

Across the street, Zahir was standing by the open garage door wiping oil off a car part. Elaina looked up and saw him. He waved tentatively at her and she nodded back.

"Let me drive you home," Elaina said. "I'll go tell Pop."

That night as they were closing up the diner, Zahir stopped in.

"Hi Elaina. I just wanted to tell you that the pie you gave me was so delicious. I had to fight Malik and Arif away from it."

She smiled. "I'm glad you liked it. I've got some extra pecan pie tonight. Would you like a piece?"

"I've never had it before."

Elaina boxed up a slice for him. "Here. I think you'll like it.

And by the way, you did an awesome job on my car's alignment. I hadn't realized how bad it was. Thanks so much, again." He smiled shyly then scuffed the floor with his boot.

"Listen. I saw your friend, that gallery man, crying this afternoon. Is everything OK?"

"Rhey's friend Robbie died in the World Trade Center. His friend called today to tell Rhey that they've identified his remains."

Zahir's face turned grim.

"All that was left was his jawbone and lower teeth."

Zahir winced, shook his head and looked down.

"How can people commit such atrocities and say it's in the name of God? Please tell your friend I'm very sorry, Elaina."

"Thanks, I'm sure he'll appreciate your kind words."

Rhey was sitting cross-legged on the gallery floor in the dark drinking strong rum when Elaina let herself in.

"Robbie loved Jamaican rum. He brought me this back from his last cruise. I haven't had the heart to open it before now. What time is it, El?"

"A quarter to nine."

"Oh, El. I don't think I can do the candle slideshow tonight. Do you think people will hate me? Or be disappointed in me?"

"Rhey, don't worry. You're grieving. I think people will understand once they find out why. By the way, Zahir came over tonight. He wanted to thank me for the pie I baked him, but I really think it was because he wanted to see how you were. He saw us at the picnic table."

"Really? Zahir did? How sweet of him." He raised the bottle of rum. "To Zahir, my favorite jihadist in the 'hood."

"You've got to stop saying that. He's a good guy. I can tell."

"You're right. Ooh, I feel so guilty about the candle thing," he said as he swigged more rum.

"Do you have something else you could display? A photo of Robbie?"

"Elly—*wondrous* idea. Here, hold the rum." Rhey thrust the bottle into her hands as he stumbled off to his apartment. She could hear him dropping things on the floor, and cupboards and drawers opened roughly then slammed shut.

"Found it, Elly. This is perfect! Come on, it's show time."

She joined him in the projection booth as he scanned the image onto the computer and cropped it to be displayed.

At 9:11 p.m., Robbie's image grinned back at them from the drive-in screen. He was leaning on the rail of a cruise ship, with the sun setting over the Caribbean behind him. He was buff, tanned perfectly and wore nothing but puka shells around his neck and white drawstring pants.

"Wow, he *was* an Adonis," Elaina said.

"Give me that rum, Elly."

* * *

Over the next couple of months, paranoia destroyed what little common sense remained. One day in May, Elaina noticed a group of customers gathered around a man in a booth who was folding a $20 bill. She grabbed the coffee pot and did a refill sweep so she could hear what was going on.

"I learned this in an e-mail I got yesterday. You take a $20 bill—a newer one printed after 1998—and hold it with the back facing you. Now fold up the bottom half of the bill away from you. Then take the left half and fold it up vertically behind the bill like this. Now repeat with the other side. OK, folks, are you ready for this?" He flipped over the bill that looked like an unfinished paper airplane.

"Look at that. These are the Twin Towers as they looked after being hit by the planes on 9/11. See the one on the right is the North Tower if you're looking south from midtown Manhattan. See that 'smoke' pouring out of both towers? The North Tower's smoke is higher up, 'cause it was hit above the 90th floor and the South Tower was hit in the 40s."

The crowd gasped.

"And it gets spookier, folks. See the words here on the sides of the bill? America and United. The planes that hit the towers were American and United airliners."

"You forgot the Pentagon," his wife said.

"Oh yeah, look at this." He flipped over the bill and the folded image resembled smoke billowing out of the Pentagon after it was hit.

"But if that bill was printed in 1998, how could this imagery be on the $20 bill?" a woman asked.

Elaina heard a voice moving behind her. "The Illuminati." She turned around and saw that American Indian who'd left the aluminum foil sculpture as a tip on 9/11 walk past her and sit in the last booth.

"He's right," the man with the $20 bill said. "The Illuminati are the elite rich who secretly run this world.

They're part of the New World Order."

The man in the last booth nodded at the group.

"They *think* they run this world, but the Creator has some big surprises for them." He held up his sachet of tea to Elaina and she came over with a pot of hot water and took his order.

Elaina kept her ears tuned to the conversations about the $20 bill trick and other dire predictions rampant on the Internet. As she brought other customers their orders, she overheard phrases such as "suitcase nukes," "biological warfare" and "a strike on our power grids."

"Everyone just has to stay alert. Especially out here in the country by the airport," the man with the $20 bill said. "This would be a perfect area for a terrorist training camp."

She thought about the mechanic from across the street, Zahir. Did he injure himself on purpose that day last fall so he could case the joint for some act of terror? Was his rescue of her after the accident a way to ingratiate himself to her?

"Your customer is at the cash register," Angie said to her. Elaina went over and took the American Indian's check and money. She handed him his change.

"*Nyawéñha,*" Simon said as he grabbed more cinnamon toothpicks.

Elaina almost asked him what that meant but was intimidated by his solemn expression. As soon as he got into his pickup, she went to the booth to clean up. Again, there was no tip but this time she found a little sculpture on the table top. It was of a man sitting cross-legged on a skull and crossbones. It gave her the creeps.

She stopped by the gallery on the way home to visit Rhey during his candle slideshow. He'd gotten such positive feedback from the community—and people had come to the gallery specifically because they'd heard about what he was doing—that he decided to keep showing it until the first anniversary of 9/11. They sat in the projection booth eating pecan pie and sipping hot rum coffee talking about their day. An evening breeze stirred up dandelion seed heads in the field surrounding the movie screen. Some of the wisps strayed into the path of the projection beam, becoming part of the art. They were falling lives. Falling hopes. Falling dreams.

"I wish you hadn't told me about that $20 bill business," Rhey laughed. "I thought I couldn't possibly be more paranoid. Wrong!"

"Have you ever heard of the Illuminati? This American Indian who comes in every once in a while said they were behind 9/11. They control everything. They're the rich powers running the world behind the scenes."

"Never heard of them, although that name gives them a certain Machiavellian elegance."

Elaina nodded, pretending that she understood the reference. Sometimes it was difficult to keep up with Rhey. "Oh, I almost forgot to tell you something else about that guy. Twice I've waited on him and he's left me no tip. Instead he leaves these creepy sculptures made out of aluminum foil."

"Props to him for using a unique medium," Rhey nodded. "Are they any good?"

"They're little figures riding things. I should bring them

over for you to see. You'd get a kick out of them."

"If he's any good, maybe I can get him to hold a show here. The medium sounds a tad avant-garde in a folk art way. It might make some galleristas go gaga."

"Whatever you say, Rhey."

Suddenly they were startled by what sounded like gunshots close by. They jumped straight up in their seats at the same time. The coincidence made them laugh uncontrollably.

"I've got jihadists in my 'hood. Somebody, save me, *please*!" Rhey begged. "C'mon! What hunting season could it possibly be this time of year?"

Elaina shrugged. "I dunno. Wild turkey? Naaah. It's probably just the jihadists up the road." She patted his arm. "Don't worry. The pie maker will protect ya."

"Did you *hear* that, jihadists? Back off, or she'll flute your crusts!"

~ Chapter 4 ~

Dark dreams lingered.

Here it was January 2003 already and Elaina's nights were still haunted by the image of that stranger pulling her from the Twin Towers. Surely the details she'd learned months ago of Robbie's death didn't help her shed the frightening vision. Who was the man in blue? She looked across the street that morning wondering if the blue symbolized Zahir's eyes. Her thoughts were interrupted when that American Indian man came in carrying his rucksack and sat in his usual booth.

She brought hot water over and a menu, but he rejected the latter.

"Fasting," he said. Elaina wondered why he'd bother to come into a diner if he was fasting, but she left him alone to his sachet of tea and hot water. Despite not ordering food, the man lingered in the booth and almost looked as if he were in some sort of trance. Should she offer him more water, she wondered. Or was it wiser to stay back? An hour later she was at the cash register when the man finally got up to leave. He opened the door, turned around to her and said, *"Nyaweñha...Thank you,"* then left. She went to the booth, picked up the mug and found a $20 bill folded to show the burning Twin Towers. On the seat was another sculpture: two men, one balding and wearing glasses, riding a snake. She unfolded the twenty, stuck it in her apron pocket and carried the sculpture out back to the shelf with the others.

Business at the diner was improving and almost back to what it was before the attacks. Traffic at the airport was another story. Passengers had to go through new security procedures that seemed to change every day. Surprising items were banned. Who would have thought a nail clipper would be considered a terrorist weapon? It was crazy.

The night President Bush was going to give his State of the Union Address, Elaina was in no mood for Iraq war talk. She stopped by the gallery after work to try a new daiquiri flavor Rhey was pulsing in the blender. He poured the libation, the color of a pale ocean sunset, into martini glasses and garnished them with skewered cubes of mango.

"Let's have a slideshow tonight, Elly. I'm bored."

"Good idea."

Rhey assembled a random collection of new and old photos and scanned them into the projector's computer. He opened a bag of tortilla chips and poured them into a bowl next to the salsa.

"I have an idea," he said scooping up salsa. "Let's pretend the projector is a Magic 8 Ball. We'll ask a question, hit the advance button on the picture show and see what the big picture answer is. Sound fun?"

Elaina nodded as she sipped her daiquiri.

"You go first, El." She grinned. Of all the questions she could ask, what would be the perfect one for that moment?

"What will I be doing a year from now?"

"OK, now hit the magic button."

A close-up of one of her lemon meringue pies spread across the screen. Rhey laughed; Elaina frowned.

"Did you set me up for this?"

"No, I swear. Now me. Let's see," he said as he closed his eyes and crossed his fingers. "What will *I* be doing a year from now?" He tapped the button and an image of Zahir in his mechanic's uniform shone on the screen next. "I'd jihad that!"

"Get that off of there. What if he sees it from his house?" Elaina said.

"Hah! OK, magic screen, give me another answer." This time a photo of a cruise ship appeared.

"Now you're talkin'," Rhey grinned as he poured another drink.

"My turn. Will I travel anywhere this year?" Elaina asked. The reply was an image of the Binghamton skyline.

"Ugh. I hate this game already."

Rhey set his drink down.

"Listen up, Elly. It's time for a mini-intervention here. I think the magic screen is trying to tell you, and I concur, that you need to start taking more chances in your life. Be spontaneous! Seriously. You've got to expand your horizons beyond this two-bit town," he said pointing at the screen. "Why don't you wear a low-cut red dress once in a while? Wear seamed stockings to work. Go streaking down Court Street."

She blushed. "Uh, like I would *ever* do any of those things."

"See. My point, I mean *our* point (as he gestured at the

screen) exactly. You're not a bad-looking gal. You've got a bod you could work a bit more, and that hair would benefit from some serious product in it. We should take you to the makeup counter at the mall for one of those free makeovers."

"Your turn," she said as she folded her arms.

"Yes, back to my fabulous life. What will be the subject of my next big art opening here?"

The reply was a photo of Elaina's work space in the diner. A baked pie sat next to an open box of aluminum foil.

"Oh, I forgot to tell you. That Indian came back and left another sculpture. I didn't get to ask his name though. Next time."

"Big help you are. Next question."

Elaina folded her hands in front of her face.

"Will I meet the man of my dreams this year?"

"She means besides me, oh magic screen of wonder."

The photo was a designer blue jeans ad taken from a magazine. A handsome man wearing tight jeans and an unbuttoned blue shirt held a newborn lamb in his arms.

"Um, magic screen of wonder, I think that was meant for me," Rhey said leaning forward wagging his drink. He crunched a tortilla chip.

Elaina stared at the image, wide-eyed.

"No...this is definitely meant for me. I've been having these recurring dreams since 9/11. I'm in the burning towers and trapped in a stairwell. A hand reaches out, from a man I can't see through the black smoke, and he pulls me safely outdoors where the sun is shining. I never see his face, but he's always wearing a blue shirt."

"So that lamb might be you?"

She shrugged. "What am I being saved from?"

Rhey looked at his friend, whom he loved dearly. He knew she'd never have the choices or experiences that he'd already had in his life. This was where she was planted and would probably remain, making pies until her last breath.

"Maybe the dream means good fortune is coming to you very soon." He smiled and patted her hand. She thought about what he said and smiled. "Yeah, maybe you're right."

Not long after, the war began in Iraq. Some of the customers asked Walt to turn on the TV so they could watch the "Shock & Awe Show" live as they ate their hot turkey sandwiches with gravy and apple pie for dessert, of course. Mary Jo had been better about reporting to work these days, so Elaina was happy to spend most of her work day in the kitchen, away from the violent TV footage. One day Angie called in sick after she tripped on the steps to her apartment and broke her front tooth. That was the day the American Indian returned.

"I'll take him," Elaina said to Mary Jo. She carried the pot of hot water to his booth and this time asked if he wanted the menu before handing it to him. He did take it and ordered the day's side dish, squash, and a cup of the corn chowder.

"What do you think of all that," she said pointing at the TV screen.

"Stupidity."

"By the way, I've been meaning to tell you I love those

sculptures you've left me here. The detail is amazing." He nodded and dunked his herbal tea sachet.

"My name's Elaina."

He looked up as he stirred the sachet with his finger.

"I can see."

"What's your name?"

"Simon."

She wanted to ask him for his last name but sensed he wanted to be left alone.

"Rhey, it's me," she whispered into the phone. "That aluminum foil sculptor is here. Why don't you stop by and introduce yourself? You could bring some gallery flyers and pretend you're dropping them off here."

"What should I say to him?"

"Maybe he'll strike up a conversation with you about the art. I don't know. His name is Simon, by the way."

"OK, I'll be up."

Simon waved Elaina back to his booth.

"I'd like some pie."

"We have apple, blueberry, peanut butter fluff and chocolate cream. What would you like, Simon?"

"You choose."

She went out back and looked at the pies. Was this some type of test? She tried to recall what he'd eaten there before to see if she could figure out what his taste was like. All she could remember was that tea he'd bring. What was the best pie she'd made today? Everyone was going for the apple, but she linked that to the underlying theme of everything patriotic these days.

If she gave him a slice of apple pie would he be offended, since he appears to disagree with our war in Iraq? Maybe if she did eenie-meenie-miney-moe? Unfortunately, that came back to the apple. *Why is it so hard for me to make decisions?* She sighed and then grabbed a slice of blueberry to bring to him.

Simon smiled. "My favorite."

Elaina sat on a stool behind the cash register tapping a pen against the wall. Where is Rhey? He's going to miss meeting Simon. It was too late. Simon was already at the cash register, handing her the check and his money.

"Thank you, Elaina. Good pie." He grabbed some toothpicks, pushed open the door, and then looked back at her.

"I hope your friend enjoys the cruise."

Thanks, I guess, she thought. Simon was gone by the time Rhey arrived.

"Where have you been? What kept you so long? You just missed him."

"I got a phone call I've been waiting for. Sorry, El. Hey, did he leave you any art?"

"Oh, I forgot to check." Sure enough. Next to the plate was a sculpture of a man riding an anchor. She waved Rhey over and handed it to him. "Come back in the kitchen and I'll show you the others."

Rhey was very impressed with the details Simon could get in the faces of the tiny figures. That was quite a feat with a clunky medium like aluminum foil.

"Wow, this *is* great folk art. I'd love to exhibit his work. You didn't get his last name?"

"I was afraid to," she laughed. "He's kinda grim. Didn't want to push him."

"Chicken."

"When he left, he told me to tell my friend to enjoy the cruise."

Rhey's jaw dropped. "Whaaaaat?"

"Why, are you going on a cruise or something?"

"Well, the phone call that delayed me was from a travel agent. I didn't tell you this but my Aunt Tillie has been very concerned about me since Robbie's death. She won a month-long tour of the Mediterranean in May and wants to cheer me up by taking me along."

"Really? That's so awesome."

"I know, though it's too close to the Middle East for my comfort. I wish she'd won a cruise to Hawaii. Oh well, beggars can't be.... Maybe I could fit you in my suitcase Elly," he said with a shrug. She wished she could tag along, too. It sounded so exotic. The furthest she'd been from home was going to Lisa's family's cabin in the Thousand Islands. A couple of years ago she went to her cousin's wedding in Scranton and had a really good time, but that was about it.

"We're flying from JFK to Barcelona. I'm certainly not thrilled about all the air time. Think I'll have to self-medicate with serious amounts of rum and a halcyon chaser to cross the Atlantic. Then we'll pick up the first cruise boat that takes us to Monte Carlo, Venice and Rome. The second cruise will focus on the Greek Isles: Corfu, Santorini, Mykonos and Crete. We'll stop for a brief stay on Ibiza then it's back to Barcelona and home. I'll come back all tan and gorgeous. You'll hardly recognize me."

"Greece? That's so cool. My grandparents came from Patras. Will you be near there?" She tried to act enthused for Rhey, but the news hit her hard. What would she do for a whole month without him? They spent more time together recently than some married couples. Who would she hang out with? What would she do on Friday nights if there wasn't a picture show? She wasn't looking forward to hanging out with Lisa on weekends again at Cubby's metalheads meat market.

"What about the gallery?"

"I'll just shutter it for the time I'm away. No biggie." Elaina laughed to herself. If they shut down the diner for a month, it would have a huge impact on their lives. But when you're born into money, as Rhey was, that was never a concern.

"I'm really going to miss you." Elaina pouted.

"I'll be back before you know it. And if you promise to wear some makeup and use the product I got you for your hair every day, I'll bring you back a real Grace Kelly scarf from Monaco."

That thought lit up Elaina's smile. An elegant scarf from the Mediterranean would definitely be worth the wait.

His May departure date arrived sooner than Elaina would have liked and she bade Rhey a teary farewell. She wasn't looking forward to a month without the joy he brought into her life. How she wished she could see the Mediterranean for herself. Maybe someday.

That Tuesday, Mary Jo called to say she couldn't come in because both little Jimmy and their dog Wolfgang ran into the stinky side of a skunk. Argh, Elaina thought. Not again. Angie was depressed—something Elaina and Walt were not used to seeing. She'd gotten the dentist's bill for having a crown put on her broken front tooth and was worried about how she'd be able to pay for it, even with the installment payment plan.

To add to the day's misery, it was hotter than normal out and the diner's air conditioning wasn't working. The diner was packed by late afternoon and everyone was complaining about how warm it was inside. In the first booth by the door, a young mother was trying to keep four young children controlled while they ate dinner. The baby was screeching at a pitch that could only signify the impending arrival of a new tooth. Two of the boys were pinching each other, and their mother kept reaching across the table to swat them. The other boy unscrewed the top of the salt shaker and poured its contents on the floor. Elaina saw the mess, right in line with all the foot traffic into the diner, so she scurried over with a carpet sweeper to clean it up.

The sweeper wasn't picking anything up. She flipped it over and saw something snagged in the bristles. Elaina bent down to remove the debris just as the boy unscrewed the top of the pepper shaker and dumped it on her head. It fell in slow motion like ashes around her face and for a second, she couldn't see. A man reached out his hand to help her up, and when she stopped sneezing, she was so struck by his handsomeness she didn't know what to say and just stared. Then she realized she was still holding his hand and let go of it like a robber caught with a bag of diamonds.

"You OK, miss?"

"Anthony! You apologize to that waitress right now! I'm so sorry. I can't believe how horrible my kids are behaving."

Elaina shook the pepper out of her hair, frowned at the booth of chaos, wiped her sweaty brow and then looked back at the man in the blue sailor's shirt.

"Yeah, I'm OK," Elaina said finally. "Thanks. We're kinda full right now, do you mind sitting at the counter?"

"Sure. No need for a menu. Give me a coke, medium rare cheeseburger and some freedom fries."

The sailor parked his duffle bag next to the stool. A man to his right smiled.

"You back from the front, son?"

"Yessir. Can't say where I've been because of the nature of my deployment, but yes, fighting the war on terror. Just flew in from Virginia."

"My nephew's in the Navy, too. He's on a carrier somewhere in the Persian Gulf."

"Good for him."

The man leaned over toward the sailor. "You think we're going to win this thing?"

"Yessir. Mission's accomplished and freedom's on the march. What we need to be concerned about now is the threat already among us."

"I agree, son."

Elaina brought him his order and then stopped to refill the coffee makers. She listened to their conversation, with her back to the two men, as the sailor talked about his travels around the world. How she'd love to do something like that—like Rhey was doing right now. What must it be like to try exotic cuisines and travel where no one spoke English?

When the older man went to pay his tab, he handed Elaina an extra twenty.

"I'd like to buy that patriot his dinner, Elaina. Give him anything he wants." The man saluted the sailor and walked out the door.

"Well, you heard what he said. Can I get you anything else?"

"Since it's on his dollar, I'd love a piece of pie. Do you have any fruit pies?"

"How's apple sound?"

"You read my mind, honey."

Elaina blushed as she went out back for the pie. Walt noticed her pink cheeks and smiled. He looked out the order window at the sailor.

"I can take it to that sailor fella," he said taking the piece of pie out of her hands.

"But...." Elaina sighed.

"Here you go, son. Hi, I'm the owner, Walt Brady. Home on leave?"

"Petty Officer Third Class Mitch Johnson. Nice to meet you." From the strength of his grip, Walt knew this man was no paper pusher. "Just finished a tour of duty."

"Where've you been?"

"I can't disclose that sir. Special Ops," he whispered. "I

was part of the rescue and recovery at the Pentagon on 9/11. After that, I was deployed in the war on terror."

"Thank you for your service, son. Did you lose friends at the Pentagon?"

"No, sir. Did see some buddies injured when I was deployed. Luckily, we all came home alive."

Mitch took a big bite of the apple pie and sighed.

"Now that there's America, right there in that delicious morsel."

"My daughter Elaina bakes the pies. Did you meet her yet?"

"Was that her at the front door."

"Elaina," Walt called, "there's someone here I'd like you to meet."

She blushed as she shook his hand.

"Well my, my, Miss American Pie. You sure can bake like a dream, Elaina. I don't know, Walt. I might just have to marry this daughter of yours."

Walt elbowed Elaina and she elbowed him right back.

"I have some work out back. Nice meeting you, Mitch."

Mitch watched her walk away. The girl wasn't much of a looker, he thought, but boy could she bake great pie. It'd be worth his time to make this place a frequent stop.

Elaina asked her father if she could get out of work early Thursday to shop at some of the pre-summer sales at the Mall. The day that cute sailor came in she was wearing a blouse so old it was threadbare around the hem. What if he came by again? Elaina didn't want him to see her looking like that. She tried to remember all the advice Rhey gave her about the most flattering ways to use clothes to show off her body. As she was looking at a rack of casual dresses on sale in the department store across from the shop where her friend worked, Elaina saw Lisa run out into the hallway and jump into Lenny's arms, legs wrapped around his waist. He spun like a top until she looked dizzy and then they kissed each other passionately, oblivious to the shoppers who paused to stare.

"Can you believe it?" Lisa yelled as she hopped up and down. Lenny nodded and then he grabbed her again with his burly arms for one more intense lip lock. Lisa waved goodbye and ran back into the clothing store.

Elaina wondered what that was all about. She had planned to visit Lisa's store after she finished shopping, but after that dramatic display, it was too difficult to focus on finding a dress now. She let curiosity drag her out of the department store and push her reluctantly into Lisa's shop.

"Hey? Got any bargains in here?" Elaina waved at Lisa, who looked up from the cash register expressionless when she entered.

"Nothing you'd ever wear."

"Or so you think," Elaina grinned but Lisa's face was unmoved.

"How come you're not at the diner?"

"I asked Pop for some time off. Need to get some new wardrobe essentials."

"'Wardrobe essentials'—man, you've been hanging out with that old guy too much."

"Rhey's not old! He's like 30 something."

Lisa shook her head. "Yeah, right. More like 40 something."

"Whatever. I don't care if he's older; he's a great guy and a good friend." Elaina wanted to add, better than you've ever been to me, but bit her lip. "Anyway, what's new, Lisa? Feel like going to Cubby's on Saturday?"

Lisa folded a pile of studded T-shirts. "I dunno. Might have plans that night."

"Oh, like going out of town or something? Does Lenny have a gig somewhere?"

Lisa stared at Elaina's outfit for a moment. *Did she ever buy anything current or that fit right? She should live in Iowa or someplace, 'cause her outfit screams "I'm a freakin' farm girl." D'oh, like doesn't she know I just hang around her when I'm bored? Seriously, what a no-lifer.*

"Yeah. But there's only room in the van for me. Sorry." Lisa put her head down and continued folding as if Elaina had already left.

Great, Elaina thought as she walked across the mall parking lot to her car. Soon there'll be no one to hang out with.

Saturday morning Mary Jo called in with another family emergency. This time it was a leaking water heater and Merle was out of town. Elaina was mad. She'd be closing the diner on a Saturday night again. No friends, no social life, no fun! Would she ever have a life outside of this damn diner? As she reset a table, someone tapped her shoulder. She spun around, teeth clenched, and was shocked to see her sister Dee Dee.

"*Sis?*" Elaina's jaw dropped as they hugged. "What the...what are you doing here?"

"Go into the kitchen. I have something to tell you and Pop. I'll meet you two in there."

"OK. But what's with the mystery?"

"Go on," Dee Dee said, shooing Elaina away. Dee Dee looked out the front window and waved to a young man waiting outside in the parking lot. They walked into the kitchen holding hands. Elaina looked at the young man standing next to her sister. He had tousled black curls and a shy, but cute, grin.

"Pop. Sis. I'd like you to meet Joachim. I mean, this is my *husband,* Joachim."

"*What?*" Walt said as he raised one eyebrow. It was a gesture he displayed to his daughters when they were caught doing something wrong.

"You're *married?*" Elaina gasped.

"Yes!" Dee Dee said putting her hand up to display her ring. "Before you say anything, let me explain. Joachim is from Germany. We've known each other since freshman year. He plays the cello, too. He wants to go to grad school, as I do, and his visa was about to expire. After 9/11, it's become more complicated to get your visa renewed, and we have this fantastic teacher right now, and it's important not just for our lives but our careers, so we got married by a justice of the peace."

Walt scratched his chin as he gave Joachim a close look.

"Tell me, Dee Dee. Do you love him?"

She blushed. "Yes. Of course! We really enjoy each other's company. And, we do make beautiful music together."

"How about you, son," Walt said to Joachim. "Do you love my daughter?"

Joachim grinned. "Yes. Very, *very* much."

Those words made Elaina's heart pang. What did that feel like? Here she was the eldest daughter in the family, and at twenty-eight, she'd still never had a serious relationship. Dee Dee had already seen more of the world than her, married a foreigner and knew what it was like to make beautiful music with someone. She didn't want to allow jealousy into this moment, but it was hard to push away the reaction.

"Well," Walt said, shaking his head, "your mother and I married just for love and look where it got us. Perhaps since you've married for your careers, too, you'll have better luck. What's your last name, Joachim?"

"Bartle."

Walt extended his right hand. "Welcome to the family, son." Joachim shook his hand vigorously.

"Thank you, Herr Brady. I will take very good care of Dee Dee."

"God help you, son." Walt laughed as he patted him on the shoulder. "So, have you kids eaten yet?"

"No," Dee Dee said taking off her coat and draping it over her arm. "We're starving."

Walt gestured to them to sit down at a back table. "I'll fix you up something hearty. Tomorrow we can have a barbecue at home. I'll grill up some chicken spiedies for Joachim. Gotta give him a real taste of local cuisine."

Elaina volunteered to close up the diner so Walt could go home and spend some time chatting with the newlyweds. Truth was, she hadn't quite come to terms with her twinges of jealousy and thought if she took some time to let the news sink in, she'd be in a more festive mood. As she unscrewed the salt and pepper shaker tops to refill them, she wondered what exotic isle Rhey's cruise ship was parked next to. Had he bought her that Grace Kelly scarf yet? Was he sitting on a chaise lounge on the top deck under a starry sky, drinking a daiquiri with a little umbrella in it?

The front door opened, startling Elaina and she yelled out, "We're closed."

"Sorry, Miss Brady. I was just wondering if I could get another slice of your mouth-watering apple pie?"

It was that sailor, Mitch. He looked so different. He wore jeans that fit him in a way Rhey would appreciate, she thought. His white shirt, tucked under a light leather jacket, showed off his tanned face. It took a second to catch her breath.

"Hi," she blushed. "Sure, c'mon in. Have a seat at the counter and I'll go see if we have any apple pie left. So what have you been up to?" she called out from the kitchen.

"Not much. Dreaming of another piece of your pie, mostly."

Elaina grinned as she cut the pie. Boy, if Dee Dee could be here now to hear that.

"Here you go. Want some coffee with it?"

Zahir closed the hood of the car he was working on and

grabbed a rag to wipe oil spilled on the wrench. He looked across the road and saw Elaina in the diner with a stranger. Walt's car was gone. He knew the diner should have been closed by now. Maybe I should see if everything's OK, he thought. He washed his hands, tucked in his shirt, combed his hair back with his fingers and crossed the road.

"Well hi, Zahir. I suppose you're here looking for some pie, too."

"Yes, thank you Elaina. I was just getting ready to leave and was surprised to see the lights still on." He looked at Mitch. "And then I thought, oh good, maybe I can get some apple pie."

"You're in luck. Have a seat. One last slice out back."

Zahir nodded at Mitch. "Hi, how are you this evening?"

Mitch glared back.

"Mitch here just returned from the war front. He's just like you, loves that apple pie of mine." Zahir nodded at him.

"That's right," Mitch said, standing so his 6'3" frame cast a shadow over Zahir. "I love everything *American*." He put a $5 bill on the counter. "Keep the change, Elaina. I'll see you again." Elaina blushed. Zahir's heart sank. What could she see in a jerk like that? He waited for Mitch to pull away before he spoke.

"I'll be honest, Elaina. I saw you alone over here with a stranger and I got worried. You know, I'm always across the street if you ever need me."

"Thanks. That's so kind of you to say. It's nice to know there are good neighbors always watching out for me."

"Where's Walt this evening?"

"My sister came home with a surprise today—a husband! She up and got married to this guy she goes to music school with. He seems real nice. Pop wanted to spend some time with them tonight, to get to know him better."

"A wonderful surprise. Blessings on your family for this happiness."

He waited until she was done cleaning up and walked her to the car.

"Remember, I'm here if you need me."

~ Chapter 5 ~

Love can surprise.

Elaina wasn't the only person who felt a twinge of jealousy at Dee Dee and Joachim's marriage. Walt tried to recall the feelings he and Maria shared back when they met at that dance senior year in high school. He was definitely the shy Irish boy, and exotic Maria had coaxed him out onto the dance floor as the band covered the Allman Brothers' "Ramblin' Man." His buddies laughed from the sidelines as Walt shuffled awkwardly while Maria twirled like a carefree hippie around him. God, she was beautiful with her straight honey-colored hair and tiny waist. Even though his friends were laughing, they were insanely jealous.

That night, before the dance was over, she'd led him under the stands in the stadium where they made out. Sure, he'd kissed a few girls in his class, but Maria was different. She was experienced and when they kissed, he felt a deep, soulful connection to her. Thoughts of going away to that state college to study architecture faded. It was as if he knew at that moment their lives were forever intertwined. A year later she was carrying Elaina and Walt had to find a full-time job quickly. His parents were ashamed of his actions and the consequence. They responded by kicking him out of the house.

He'd worked part-time in high school slicing onions and

washing dishes at the Chinese take-out on Main Street. That helped him get a job as a short-order cook at Maria's father's diner. A few years after they married, he and Maria took out a loan to buy the diner from Metro. And like that, his destiny was sealed. Walt often wondered what his life might have been like if he'd never met Maria and went to architecture school instead.

"I like Joachim," Elaina said Monday morning as she lifted a crust into a pie pan. "They seem so happy together."

"I like him, too. Nice kid. Dee Dee agreed to a proper celebration with our family and friends once they finish off the summer semester. Probably we'll have it here sometime in September."

"That'd be nice."

"After all, she's my first daughter to get married."

As soon as he said the words, Walt noticed the joy drain from Elaina's face. He went over and draped his arm around her shoulder.

"Don't you worry now, Elaina. Your time will come soon enough. I think that sailor took a fancy to you. Sure loved your apple pie."

That restored her smile.

"I know. He came by Saturday night as I was closing up. Wanted another slice."

Walt raised an eyebrow, and then smiled when he saw how happy she looked talking about him. In the back of his mind he felt a twinge of concern. Why didn't Mitch come around during the day, when he was there?

After the lunchtime rush, the phone rang. Elaina picked up and heard the sound of a wave crashing on shore.

"Hell-ooo! Hear that, El? That's the sound of paradise calling you."

"Rhey! How are you?"

"Oh, working hard, you know. Someone has to sit here on a beach sipping a daiquiri while making sure the sun sets properly over the Mediterranean. By the way, the daiquiris on this island are so large they should be illegal. I'm sitting here alone. Aunt Tillie's in the Jacuzzi back on the ship with some Croatian gentleman so I figured it was the perfect time to read a little Graham Greene and catch up with my favorite protégé. How's life on your end of the universe?"

"You'll *never* guess what happened. Dee Dee got married!"

"Your sister in Boston? *Shocker*! Did I miss a party?"

"Not yet. We're planning one in September. Anyway, he's a music student too and his name is Joachim. He's from Germany. They got married in Boston by a justice of the peace. Came down here Saturday to surprise us."

"What spurred this deliciously impulsive behavior?"

"Joachim's visa was about to expire and renewals are more complicated since 9/11. It was a way to keep him here."

"Any love, or is this a soulless union?"

"Oh no, they definitely love each other. It's so obvious."

"You know, El, you could learn a lot from your sister's spontaneity."

"Yeah, right, like I could ever...."

Elaina's eye caught a florist delivery van pulling up and a

man came in carrying a gorgeous bouquet of red roses.

"Who's that for?" Walt said looking out the order window.

"Hold on a sec, Rhey," Elaina said as the delivery man approached her.

"Is Elaina Brady here?"

"I'm Elaina."

"These are for you. Enjoy." She was stunned. No one had ever sent her flowers. Elaina mumbled thanks to the driver.

"What's going on over there?" Rhey yelled into the phone.

"Uh...I just got a bouquet of red roses."

"Are you kidding? From whom?"

"Let me open the envelope here." Her hands shook as she pulled out the little card inside and read it to herself: *To my Miss American Pie from your favorite sailor.* Elaina gasped.

"Who sent them, Elly?"

"Ohmigod!" She danced around with the phone in her hand.

"I'm dying here. Tell me!"

"*Ohmigod, Rhey!* This guy I just met. He's a sailor and just back from the war. His name is Mitch Johnson."

"Hmm, not crazy about the porn star name. Is he handsome? Is he nice?"

"Uh-huh, uh-huh," she nodded staring at the bouquet in shock.

"What's going on over there? I leave Binghamton and a week later all hell breaks loose. Dee Dee's married and you're hooking up with a sailor?" Rhey saw a waiter walking toward him on the beach and waved. "Oh *garçon*, I need another *grande* daiquiri, *tout de suite!*"

Walt came out of the kitchen and saw Elaina staring at the bouquet.

"They're from *Mitch*, Pop. Can you *believe* it?"

"Who?"

"You know, that sailor."

Walt nodded. "Oh. Hmm. Very nice." Walt got a kick out of seeing Elaina aglow from this public romantic gesture Mitch made, but as a man he wondered what that fellow was up to. He barely knew his daughter and a dozen, long-stem red roses weren't cheap.

"Listen, gotta run, Rhey. See you in three weeks."

"Love ya, El. Remember, I want all the details of this torrid affair when I return. Oh, and wait 'til you see the photos I've been taking for our next picture show. They'll make you feel as if you came along with me. Now remember what the magic screen told you about taking chances...."

When Elaina was done for the night she walked out to her car and was startled to see Mitch leaning against it.

He sang to her with arms outstretched, "Well hi, my Miss American Pie."

She blushed. "Thanks for the gorgeous roses. I love them."

"Well then, where's my thank-you kiss?"

She approached him tentatively and leaned awkwardly on her tiptoes to give him a light peck on his cheek. He grinned at her.

"Let's take a ride," he said pointing at his motorcycle. Elaina had never ridden on one and was afraid to admit it.

"Um, I dunno." She grinned shyly as she nibbled her fingernail.

"C'mon. Just a quick spin up to the airport and back."

Walt was still inside and she didn't know whether or not to ask him if she should go. Then she thought, what's the matter with me? I'm 28 years old. She could hear Rhey in her mind saying "Be spontaneous!"

"OK, but just up and back."

Mitch handed her a helmet, sat down and helped her onto the motorcycle.

"Now wrap your arms around my waist. *Real* tight."

She'd never hugged a man like this before and it felt weird because he was someone she barely knew. But he was sooo good looking. Only an idiot would refuse. The light wind shifted and she smelled his cologne. She imagined it was a scent you'd smell on an ocean breeze and thought, ohmigod, if Rhey could see me now.

Zahir saw the motorcycle speed out of the parking lot. It was that sailor he didn't like with Elaina. Walt was still inside working. He thought about crossing the road to let him know what his daughter was up to. Then he thought he might cause Elaina trouble and didn't want to do that. It would be better to wait around there until she returned safely.

She couldn't hear anything except the roar of the motorcycle and wind rushing past her helmet. Mitch drove up to the airport entrance then turned around as he promised. But then, instead of turning back down Airport Road toward the diner, he turned in the opposite direction onto Knapp Road and headed toward the landfill.

"Where are we going?" Elaina yelled above the noise but either he couldn't hear her or he was ignoring her. For a second, she wondered if he was abducting her. What should she do? If she tried to jump off the motorcycle would she be killed?

Down the road, Mitch slowed and pulled onto the shoulder beneath girders supporting the airport's blinking blue runway approach lights. "Wanna try something fun?" he said as he grabbed a blanket from the satchel on the back of the bike. "Come with me." He took her hand and led her across a dark field to the base of the gravely slope where the runway started. He spread out the blanket as she noticed a jet making its approach from the west.

"C'mon. lay back and watch the plane descend over us. It'll give you a real rush." She stood there for a second, looking at him wide eyed and wondering whether it was a good idea to lie down on the blanket next to him. What was he up to? Could she trust him?

"*C'mon*, hurry up. You're going to miss the show."

OK, here goes spontaneity, she thought as she laid her head on the blanket, feeling coarse weeds pushing back from the other side.

"Now keep looking up. And if you don't see any landing gear on the belly, start running for your life in the opposite direction as fast as you can." His laugh had a maniacal tinge to it that made her uncomfortable.

She bolted upright. This was nuts. What if something fell

off the plane and killed her? What if the plane crashed into them? What if Homeland Security was filming them on a hidden camera and thought they were terrorists? Her heart was pounding as Mitch pulled her back onto the blanket.

"No! Don't close your eyes. *Watch* it! This is what it feels like on an aircraft carrier," he yelled as the incoming roar made her shake with fear. She looked up just in time as the belly of the jet flew overhead.

"Whoooooooo!" Mitch yelled like a cowboy.

"Ahhhhhhhhh!" she shrieked.

Once the tail disappeared over the slope, he rolled on top of her and kissed her deeply. Her heart was pounding. His kiss made her feel faint. She could barely breathe from his weight on top of her. When she felt his hand slide under her shirt and cup her breast suddenly, she pushed him away with a strength that surprised her.

"No! Stop it! I want to go back to the diner."

"You sure?" he smirked. "You seemed to be having as much fun as I was. Sorry, but you look as delicious as a slice of pie lying there," he nibbled her ear which made her giggle. Then he slipped his tongue in her ear. She pushed him away again.

"No! I mean it, Mitch. I gotta get home. Pop will wonder where I am."

Mitch stood up suddenly and yanked the blanket from under her. He folded it up and strode back to the motorcycle.

Elaina followed behind, a tousled mess of emotions. Part of her loved his caresses and the danger she felt as that jet roared above them. Part of her felt *he* was dangerous. She barely knew him. Why did he think he could take such liberties with her so soon?

Mitch revved the engine as Elaina stepped off the motorcycle back at the diner. He looked back at her and shook his head.

"Thought you were a real woman, but I guess you're just a little girl needing daddy's approval for everything. Too bad." He vroomed his motorcycle down Airport Road, kicking up gravel that pinged Elaina's leg. She stood there with arms folded watching his taillights disappear. Did she just blow her once chance at love? What if she never saw him again? Why did she have to be so careful, so indecisive? Why couldn't she have maintained the impulsiveness and be more like Dee Dee?

She looked across the street and saw Zahir getting into his truck. He waved. She lifted her hand, smiled weakly and got into her car to go home.

Elaina couldn't sleep that night. The whole thing with Mitch had been like a carnival ride. It was scary and thrilling to have that jet fly so low above her. She closed her eyes and relived what it felt like to have Mitch's warm lips kiss hers. She could almost smell his cologne still on her. Why couldn't she have just relaxed and enjoyed his advances. After all, if he was after a one-night stand, why would he bother sending her that expensive bouquet?

Mitch. Mitch. Mitch. He was all she could think about at work the next day. She sniffed the roses still on the counter deeply before she went about waiting on Mary Jo's tables.

(Today's excuse: Wolfgang bit the mailman.) She hummed that song "American Pie" as she wiped down tables and put out new places settings. It would be great if Rhey called again so she could share every detail of her adventure with him. He'd be impressed, she thought. Except, of course, he'd disapprove of her reticence.

Dinnertime was busy, but she still thought about what she'd say if Mitch showed up for some pie. She'd tell him what a thrill it had been last night and that she liked his motorcycle. And his cologne. Every once in a while, as a customer gave her an order, she'd peek out the window to see if he was waiting. There was a slice of apple pie set aside, just in case, so she wouldn't disappoint him again.

Before she left work, she stopped in the rest room to brush her hair. She put on some of that pretty lipstick Rhey convinced her to buy after her mall makeover.

"See you at home, Pop."

Walt noticed her lipstick and heard her humming. He remembered how a new love made him feel happy once, too.

When she walked out into the parking lot, she looked each way but didn't see Mitch. Should she wait around? Down the road, approaching headlights were coming around the bend. She walked slowly to her car, trying to act casual, and waited to see if it was him. The car whizzed past. Should she leave or wait in the car a little bit? She sat there a few minutes feigning interest in the contents of her pocketbook.

"This is stupid," she said and started up the car. Down where Airport Road splits off toward the highway, a motorcycle passed her and took the ramp to Route 17 West. Was it Mitch? Should she follow? Of course she didn't and continued home.

Each night after work that week, Elaina waited a shorter amount of time. She was convinced she had succeeded in scaring him away permanently. Mitch was a worldly man, she thought. He had no time for the indecisiveness of a stupid small-town girl.

Friday night after work she decided to go shopping at the mall. She wished Rhey was with her. He would make her laugh and keep her mind off Mitch. Elaina stopped by the store where Lisa worked but only the manager was there.

"Lisa in?"

The manager gave her a funny look. "No. She doesn't work here anymore."

"What?" Elaina was stunned. Sure she hadn't been as close with Lisa these past few months, but she thought she would have at least called her up about this.

"Yeah, gave notice last week. Said she's moving to Portland with her boyfriend and the baby will be born out there."

"*Baby*?"

Elaina walked out of the mall feeling as if she'd just awakened from a coma. Had Lisa told her this and she wasn't paying attention because her mind was obsessed with Mitch? No way—she'd have recalled that kind of news. Moving across the country *and* pregnant—Elaina couldn't believe it. That moment she'd witnessed between Lisa and Lenny, had she just told him she was pregnant? Oh how she needed Rhey here. He could sort it all out for her.

"You ought to throw those away," Angie said the next Monday evening. "That bouquet is starting to stink up the joint."

She stared at the droopy flowers and thought they were beginning to look like her. Why did he send her those, anyway? Did he think my price was a lousy bouquet? Did he expect me to be an easy roll in the hay—*literally*, she thought. The flowers infuriated her. She threw the bouquet, vase and all, into the kitchen garbage pail.

"Bastard!"

"Uh, I didn't mean do it right now," Angie said, alarmed at Elaina's outburst.

She saw an envelope taped to her windshield when she left work that night. As she slid her finger under the seal to open it, she noticed the envelope smelled like Mitch's cologne. Inside was a card of a puppy covered by an upside down bowl of spaghetti. "Sorry about the mess I made," it said. Inside she saw Mitch's signature.

"My Miss American Pie,

"I was such a jerk the other night. Us sailors aren't accustomed to meeting real ladies like you. I think my post-traumatic stress has messed up my patience.

"I'm so very sorry. You're worth more than the biggest bouquet in the world to me.

"Please give me another chance.

"XXOO, Your Mitch."

His note was a little sloppy and written with heavy pressure. Elaina interpreted that to mean that he was sad and genuinely sorry about his behavior and missed her as much as she missed him. She held the card over her heart and grinned. There was still hope.

When she pulled into the diner parking lot early Saturday morning, Elaina was surprised to see Mitch waiting there.

"Good morning, sunshine," he said as he stepped off the motorcycle and walked over.

"Hi. I got your note. Thanks. It was sweet. I love puppies."

"You're welcome. Sorry for being such a jackass."

"Forgiven." *Tell him how you felt about that Monday night,* she told herself. *Don't mess this up again. Don't blow it!*

"That was wild the other night," she said shyly, twirling her pocketbook. "Crazy fun. Sorry I freaked about the jet."

Mitch grinned and looked at her in a way that made her blush.

"I hate to say this, but do you have any apple pie in there. It's been two weeks and I'm going crazy without tasting some of your apple pie."

"Sure, I've been keeping a slice for you," she said. *Damn, why did I say that? He's gonna think I'm too eager.*

"All right then," he said standing close as she unlocked the door.

"Have a seat. I'll warm it up in the microwave." Elaina walked through the diner turning on lights. As she went into the kitchen and opened the refrigerator to get the pie, she could smell his cologne and turned around to see him standing in the doorway. It made her catch her breath.

"Boy, you're impatient," she winked.

Mitch's face didn't respond. He just stared at her intensely.

"Truth is, Elaina, I'm not that hungry for pie right now."

"Huh?"

"But I do have a hunger that I think only you can fill." As he walked toward her, she didn't know what to do. *Stay calm. Be impulsive.*

"Not any supermodel...not any movie star...my heart is hungry for *you!*"

She gasped as he stood next to her and caressed her cheek with his hand.

"May I kiss you again? Just once. I miss the taste of your lips." She backed up and closed the refrigerator door as he pinned her against it. She knew she shouldn't let him get away with this, especially after he abandoned her that Monday night. Once he started kissing her and his strong arms squeezed her so close to him, all thoughts of resistance melted away. She held him tightly, conscious that this was a moment like something you'd see in the movies. It was as if she could hear Rhey coaching her: "Relax. Make the most of it, El."

He rubbed his cheek against hers and whispered, "You're so tasty I could eat you right up. I love you so much, Elaina."

Love? Love! He said he *loved* me, she thought. *No one...has...ever....* His unrelenting kisses made her dizzy. She was overwhelmed by his powerful passion.

"Let's run away and get married," he whispered in her ear

with his warm breath. He pulled away and started running his hands through her hair. "We can ride up to Niagara Falls tomorrow and be married Monday. Would you do this patriot that honor?"

She didn't know what to say. Her heart was pounding so fast and her thoughts racing even quicker.

Dee Dee's married. Lisa's living with Lenny in Portland and pregnant. I've got no one to hang out with except Rhey, and that can't go anywhere. Will I ever meet anyone else? What if this is the only marriage proposal I ever get? I'll be 30 soon. Ugh, so old. I don't want to be called a spinster. If I wait too long I won't be able to have kids. Mitch is handsome, brave (obviously). We'd have gorgeous kids. What do I know about him? He did apologize. And there were those roses. He must have money. Look at the way he's staring at me. This is crazy! I just want to stay in his arms forever. Be impulsive Rhey said. Wouldn't it be funny if I beat Lisa to the altar? Hah! And if I got married now, Dee Dee and Joachim's party in September could be for us, too....

In the heat of the moment, she wasn't too concerned about details someone with a cooler head might ask, such as where would they live? Did Mitch have a job? What was his family like? Instead, she thought that with this marriage, she might be able to finally lift the anchor that weighed her down to the diner and see the world as a Navy bride.

They heard her father's truck drive up out front. She had to think fast.

"Yes. *Yes!*"

"Great! Meet me here tomorrow around noon and bring your birth certificate so we can get the marriage license. Put some clothes in a backpack. We'll be in Niagara Falls by dinner and back here Tuesday as man and wife." He gave her another deep kiss that left her breathless then slipped out the back door.

"Hey, Elaina!" Walt yelled as he walked in and tapped the Irish pound note. "You left the front door unlocked."

She threw on her apron quickly and tried to smooth down her hair before he came into the kitchen.

"Sorry, Pop. Too focused on starting the pies, I guess."

"Whose motorcycle is out there?" Walt said, noticing that her cheeks were pinkish. Looks like she's wearing some more of that makeup Rhey got her, he thought.

"A motorcycle? I didn't see one."

"How could you miss it, parked right out front?"

"Maybe it was one of Zahir's customers." She couldn't believe she was lying to her father.

"Why wouldn't it be parked in his lot, then?" Walt said as he took stew meat out of the cooler. Elaina walked over and looked out the front window.

"I don't see anything out there, Pop. Whoever it was moved on."

She had trouble focusing on work that day. All she could think about was handsome Mitch—her future *husband!* Ohmigod, she wanted to dance around the diner with glee. She wanted to yell out loud that she was getting married but knew she couldn't. That would jinx the whole thing. Wait 'til Rhey hears this, she chuckled to herself.

"Why are you making so many pies today?" Angie asked.

"Our reserves are getting low. Don't want to run out of pie at a diner. That's be disastrous."

"Did you do somethin' different with your hair, hon?"

She blushed. "No, why?"

"You look quite pretty today, that's all. Nice to see you so happy. Oh, by the way, guess what happened to me? Someone paid the bill for my tooth! I got this month's bills and it said paid in full. I thought, what? This *has* to be a mistake. So I called them and they said some anonymous person paid off my balance. It's got to be someone who comes here. None of my family would ever do something like that for me. Trouble is I can't figure out who here would have done it."

Walt walked in on the conversation and smiled at them. "You afraid a tour bus is stopping here today?" he joked as he saw all the pies.

"Nope. We don't have very many backup pies. I thought this was a good day to catch up." *If only he knew the truth,* she thought.

That night as she cleaned up her work space, Elaina looked around and sighed. The next time she walked in there it would be as Mrs. Mitch Johnson.

~ Chapter 6 ~

It wasn't like Elaina.

After the 11:30 a.m. Mass, she'd left for the mall and here it was past nine that night and she hadn't returned. Walt worried. The stores would be closed there by now. Maybe she and Lisa stopped for dinner someplace or went to Cubby's to hear Lenny's band, he thought. Truth was she hadn't been hanging around Lisa much since Rhey came on the scene. Did he come home from his cruise and she was over at his gallery? Walt checked the calendar and saw he wasn't due home for another full week. Wouldn't she have called to check in with me by now?

Then his thoughts drifted to Mitch. Walt hadn't made up his mind about that fellow. He felt like he was giving his daughter the rush, especially after that showy bouquet. A dozen roses were not a cheap gesture. Mitch was a veteran. That impressed Walt. However, a sailor might be too worldly for Elaina. Her universe was much simpler. For a flicker of a second Mitch's face turned into that of the trucker from Missoula in Walt's mind. Oh no, he thought, he hoped this wasn't history repeating itself.

By ten o'clock, Walt was convinced that Elaina was somewhere with Mitch. It was the only thing that made any sense. He looked him up in the phone book but there was no listing for his name. That made Walt even more nervous.

He phoned his friend at the Sheriff's Department and explained his concern.

"Has she ever done anything like this before?" Sgt. Wilcox asked.

"No. Never. Elaina always checks in if she's going to be delayed."

"Listen, I'll take down all the information about her now and alert the deputies. Call me immediately if you hear from her, Walt."

He couldn't sleep. Should he call Dee Dee or would that worry her over nothing? Elaina had always been so reliable. Even as a teenager he always knew where she was. Walt went downstairs and sat in front of the TV. As he surfed through the infomercials and old TV shows, he winced when he came across a few police dramas that involved missing women. So what if it was 2 a.m.? He called Dee Dee and woke her up.

"No, of course she's not here, Pop," Dee Dee said, concern rising as she realized she wasn't dreaming. "I can't think of anywhere she'd be."

"Well, there's this sailor fella who started coming to the diner. He sent her flowers a week ago Monday and then she didn't hear from him again."

"Flowers?"

"Yeah, a dozen roses."

"Whoa! Oh, she must have been floored by that. I don't think any guy's ever sent her roses."

"Elaina was walking on air after the bouquet arrived.

Handsome kid. He just came back from the war. Told me he was part of the 9/11 recovery at the Pentagon, then was deployed for Special Ops somewhere he couldn't tell me. I don't know whether to believe him."

"Eeuw, this is getting creepy, Pop."

"Well, that might just be my take. The kid is very polite. Crazy about Elaina's pies, of course."

Dee Dee laughed.

"Dad...you don't suppose they eloped or something?"

Walt held the receiver to his chest. Not my Elaina, too. Lord, it's selfish, I know, he thought, but I'm so used to her being home. I don't think I could handle being alone now. Not yet.

"Pop? You there?"

"Oh no. Geez, I hope they didn't do something crazy like that. At least you knew Joachim. Elaina knows nothing about this fella."

"And she's got zip experience in the romance department which makes her extra vulnerable. Man, maybe she's just like Mom." Dee Dee regretted the words as soon as she said them. There was a long pause and Dee Dee wondered if he was crying.

"What are we gonna do, Pop? Should I come home?"

"If she doesn't come home by noon, I'll put up some posters in the diner tomorrow and ask around about Mitch. The sheriff's deputy already has the info for the missing person report. Hopefully she'll come home safe soon and with a good explanation. Actually, who cares about an explanation?"

"I wish there were Amber Alerts for adults," Dee Dee said.

Walt laughed. "People go missing all the time. The system would break, it'd be so overloaded. No one would pay attention. Like the boy crying wolf."

More silence.

"Pop, Joachim and I can cut classes tomorrow and come down."

"Let's wait and see what happens this morning first, OK? I love you, daughter."

"You too, Pop."

It was odd the next morning to enter the diner and not be greeted by the smell of Elaina's blueberry muffins baking or the smell of pared apples, sugar and cinnamon melding flavors in a bowl. That's when Walt remembered all the extra pies she was baking on Saturday. *Of course!* She was doing that because she knew she wouldn't be here this morning. This small clue lifted his spirits because it meant she was probably safe. He exhaled for the first time since he called the Sheriff's Department last night.

"What are you up to Elaina?" Walt said as he took some pies out of the freezer to bake. He even found blueberry batter ready in the refrigerator. Walt poured it into the muffin tins, popped them in the oven and started the corned beef hash.

He smiled. At least he'd done something right. Elaina cared so much about him that she left him this clue. She was OK. The question was, when would she return and what had she been up to? Since there was just enough muffin batter for this morning, did that mean she'd be back tomorrow morning?

Or, was she just trying to help him get through the first day without her?

Maria, on the other hand, had given no clues that something was going on. He had no idea she felt trapped by their marriage, stifled by her work at the diner. They always seemed to get along just fine, he thought. That trucker she ran away with—as far as he knew it was the first time he'd ever set foot in their diner. Had she met him before in secret? Or were things so bad for her that she took the first chance that came her way to get away from him? He wondered what it was about himself that was so undesirable. Did he snore loudly? Did he smack his lips when he ate? Was he selfish and uncaring toward her? He didn't think any of those things applied to him. Was it the sex? Sure things weren't what they were like back in the old high school stadium days, but she never complained. Then again, how could he miss that Maria and Elaina were so similar?

Mary Jo called in that morning saying she had a migraine. Walt was firm. "Sorry, Elaina's missing and I'm going to need all the help I can to get through today."

"What do you mean, missing?"

"Didn't come home last night. I have no idea where she is. So take some ibuprofen and get here as fast as you can."

Angie was surprised that Elaina wasn't there when she arrived. She found Walt in the kitchen, leaning over the counter with his head in his hands.

"What's goin' on? Where's the pie maker?"

"She's not here today."

"She's sick? Wow, 'cause this is the first day I ever recall her being sick. She must be lovesick."

"I said she's not *here*. I don't know where she is."

Angie put her hands over her mouth.

"Oh my Lord, Walt." She went over and gave him a big hug. "I hope Elaina didn't commit suicide over that sailor 'cause he blew her off after sending her that fancy bouquet. Oh dear, I may have caused this. I told her those flowers were stinkin' up the place."

Although Angie's pretzel logic confused Walt, something about the smell of her perfume was comforting at the moment. Didn't his mom used to wear that?

"She didn't commit suicide. I'm pretty sure of that. She's run off somewhere. I think it was something she was planning. Remember all those extra pies she was baking Saturday? She even whipped up the muffin batter for this morning."

Sgt. Wilcox stopped by the diner and Walt told him what he'd discovered in the kitchen.

"Definitely sounds premeditated. If you hear nothing by tonight, give me a call and we'll issue a statewide alert."

Zahir saw the sheriff's cruiser in the parking lot. When he noticed Elaina's car was missing, he ran over to see what was going on.

"Everything OK, Walt?"

"Hi, Zahir. Actually, no. Things are not right here. Elaina is missing."

Zahir put his hand over his heart.

"When did this happen?"

"She went to the mall yesterday around noon and I haven't heard a word from her since."

Zahir bit his lower lip. Should he tell what he knew?

"Walt, I saw her with a man in here the other night. She was closing up the diner. I came over because I didn't know if she knew this man and I wanted to make sure she was OK."

"Was he a tall fella with blond hair? Muscular?"

"Yes, that is the one. She called him Mitch. He drives the motorcycle."

"Motorcycle!" Walt remembered the one he'd seen out front of the diner Saturday morning. Then he recalled Elaina denying she'd seen it out front.

"Oh Lord, she *has* run off with that sailor."

"Who?"

"Mitch. Mitch Johnson. Dammit Elaina! What have you done?"

"She's probably married and pregnant by now. That's how those sailor boys operate," Angie said, patting Walt on the back. "I should know. My daddy was one."

Zahir was crestfallen. Gentle Elaina who'd stood up for him that day in the diner, who'd always been so kind to him, was somewhere in the arms of that surly sailor. He felt sick to his stomach. Why didn't I tell Walt sooner, he thought.

The phone rang and broke up the conversation.

"Hi Walt, it's Rhey. Just calling before my nap on deck to tell Elaina about my latest adventures."

"Well, she's got a doozy to tell you. She's not here, Rhey. In fact, I was hoping this was her."

"What do you mean not there?"

Walt turned his face away from the customers.

"I think she's run off with a fella."

"Ha-ha! That's too funny. OK, put Elaina on and tell her nice try."

Walt rubbed his forehead. "I'm not joking."

His somber tone gave Rhey the chills.

"Oh no. She really ran away? But why? With whom?"

"Well this sailor came in here a couple weeks ago. Let's see, it was just after Dee Dee and Joachim surprised us with their marriage. Zahir saw her riding a motorcycle with this fella."

"Are you kidding me? El, on a Harley? I go away and the girl goes hog wild? Oh heavens, Walt. I hope she's OK. What do you know about this guy? I hope he's not some axe-murderer type." Rhey realized what he'd just said to an already frightened Walt. Pause. Rewind, he thought. "Of course Elly's too smart for that. She'd pick up on potential axe-murderer vibes right away. Don't you think?"

"Listen, Rhey. We should probably get off the line in case she's trying to call. Enjoy the rest of your vacation. Elaina should be just fine." His voice started to break as he hung up the phone.

"From your mouth to God's ears," Rhey said as he got out of the chaise lounge and walked over to the ship's railing. He closed his eyes and pictured her riding off into the sunset with some brutish guy on a motorcycle. "Oh sweet Elly. What have you done?"

Zahir called his cousin Ahmed who was a recruiter for the U.S. Army in Dearborn, Michigan. He wondered if there was any way he could search the background of Mitch Johnson.

"Wrong branch of the service, cousin," Ahmed laughed. "I do know a recruiter for the Navy here. Let me talk with him and see if he knows someone who could do a check on this guy. I'll tell him about your concerns, with Elaina missing. That might expedite the search."

* * *

Tonight's dinner on the cruise ship had a Greek god theme. An ice sculpture of the Parthenon towered above the buffet table. The handsome waiters were all wearing togas. Normally, Rhey would have been deliriously happy with the fun festivities. Instead, his thoughts were lost somewhere an ocean away. Where was Elaina at this moment? Was she safe?

He tried to recall their last phone conversation. Had she given him any clues? Then he remembered the phone conversation interrupted by the bouquet delivery. He could hear the astonishment in her voice. He bet she never got a bouquet like that from a man before.

Poor vulnerable El, he thought as he shivered. She'd be an easy mark for a randy sailor. Then he recalled something he'd said to her about being spontaneous. "Zeus" walked by carrying a tray of Ouzo. He stopped him, took a glass and threw the drink back.

"*Yasou!*" the waiter cheered.

"*Ya*-freakin'-*sou*," Rhey said as he set the empty glass back on the waiter's tray.

Mitch and Elaina stood by the Canadian side of Niagara Falls watching its unconstrained fury roar over the horseshoe-shaped precipice. She was thinking about her father. He must be worried sick by now.

"Ready to get back to the honeymoon suite?" Mitch said with a husky tone as he drew her close, his muscled arms wrapping around her. She nodded as she noted a telephone booth next to the restrooms.

"I've gotta hit the ladies room first. I'll be right back."

"Don't take too long." Mitch smirked as he watched her walk away.

She looked back and smiled then crossed the road toward the tourist center. When he turned toward the falls, she dashed to the phone, dialed the diner's number and then pulled herself around the far side of the phone booth so Mitch couldn't see her.

Walt answered.

"Collect call from a Mrs. Mitch Johnson. Will you accept the charges?"

The news felt like a punch in the gut. Oh Lord, he thought, not Elaina, too. Why couldn't his daughters have had normal weddings, in a church, before God? Why couldn't they have given him the right to say if he approved of their choices? It had to be Maria's blood in them at work. His side of the family was never impulsive.

"Will you accept the charges?"

"Yes. Of course."

"Pop, it's Elaina. Just calling to let you know I'm OK and guess what...*ta-da*, Mitch and I got hitched. *Surprise*! Wish I could see your face right now. Ohmigod, it's so crazy! We're here in Niagara Falls and it's so beautiful. I'm so happy, Pop."

Walt hesitated before he spoke. The words wouldn't come.

"Pop, you there?"

"I'm just surprised, Elaina. Are you sure about this? Did you want to get married so soon? You hardly know Mitch."

"Oh Pop, I've never felt this way before. He's so handsome and worldly. Just swept me off my feet. I can't wait to tell Dee Dee."

So that might be it. Was this a way to catch up with Dee Dee, Walt wondered. She wanted to prove to her younger sister that she could a husband easily, too? She's right; this *is* crazy. Doesn't she know what this commitment means?

"Aren't you happy for me, Pop?"

Mitch walked over and saw her on the phone.

"Gotta run, Pop. Love ya! We'll be home tomorrow."

"What time?"

Mitch reached out from behind her and hung up the phone.

"I thought we agreed that we were going to surprise your father. We'd walk into the diner, hand in hand and have all the customers cheer."

"I know. But, I figured Pop was probably worried sick. Anyway, maybe this way he'll have a special dinner ready in our honor."

"Yeah, that'd be nice. From now on though, sugarplum,

you tell me before you do something like that again. OK?"

She nodded, but was happy that she'd called her dad with the news. Her joy made her want to stand in front of the falls and scream "I married the most handsome guy I've ever met!" Oh how she couldn't wait to see Rhey's face when he returned and saw the ring on her hand. She decided she wouldn't tell him right away, and would wait until he noticed her diamond. It wasn't a rock like something JLo would wear, but at least it was the real thing.

* * *

Walt's head pounded. A boisterous group of customers bounded in with fussy orders and all he could think about was Elaina. Thank God she called. When he phoned Sgt. Wilcox to let him know the news, it alarmed Walt when he said to call him if there was any future trouble. Did he, like Walt, sense this marriage was doomed?

As they were closing up for the evening, Walt told Angie the news. No sense in having her worry that Elaina killed herself. Angie didn't react like he expected. She sat quietly and listened carefully to his concerns.

"Listen hon, don't you be thinkin' you drove her to this, with her having a sheltered life working here at the diner and all. That's been her choice. She's a big girl. She could've gotten a job at the mall like her friend. And, secondly, from what I recall, she's not at all like your ex, Maria. Even though Elaina's married now, don't worry hon. She won't abandon you. I predict she'll still stay close by, unless that husband of hers gets redeployed. And if she does leave, well hell, you've still got

Mary Jo and me, hah-hah!" Angie brushed Walt's hand and winked at him. Oh how he loved that big toothy grin of hers.

The newlyweds arrived at the diner the next day to little fanfare. There was no special dinner waiting. No cheer from the customers. Instead, Walt and Dee Dee were waiting inside, grim-faced. Dee Dee sat on the stool and didn't get up when they came in. Walt was standing behind the counter, arms folded.

"Dee Dee? What are *you* doing here?" Elaina was stunned to see her sister. Had something bad happened? Dee Dee seemed just as shocked to see the two of them.

"I'm so glad you're here. You won't believe what's happened, Dee Dee. Look," Elaina said extending her left hand.

Dee Dee put her hand over her eyes and shook her head.

"What have you *done*, Elaina? We've been so worried." Her reaction sucked the joy from Elaina's face.

"Uh, the same thing you and Joachim did a few weeks ago."

Dee Dee looked at Mitch. He scowled back.

"It isn't the same."

Mitch pulled Elaina back to his side and draped his arm around her shoulders.

"I told you they wouldn't understand, sugarplum. They've gotta realize you're a grown woman, capable of making your own decisions. Right?"

"Yes, I am. I thought you'd all be happy for me," she said, her voice rising in pitch. "This is a big step. Mitch is wonderful.

Why aren't you happy for me?"

Walt, teeth clenched, reached his hand across the counter toward Mitch.

"Welcome to the family."

Dee Dee looked at her father then back at Mitch and held out her hand limply. Joachim came in from the kitchen carrying a tray of food for customers. He wiped his hands on the apron tied around his waist and extended his hand to Mitch.

"Hi, I'm Joachim. Dee Dee's husband." Mitch looked at him warily, but shook his hand, too.

Walt poured water into the coffee maker. "So where are you living now?"

"Mitch has a cute place in those apartments up the hill from the mall. You should see the view of the valley."

Walt looked down at the floor and collected his thoughts.

"You can gather some of your things tonight and we can help you move in completely on Sunday. I'm closing the diner early. Let's meet back at the house around 6:30 for supper."

Walt certainly wasn't in the mood to make a family dinner that night, so he brought some chili from the diner and broiled hot dogs to go along with it. The atmosphere around his kitchen table was that of a funeral luncheon, not a wedding banquet.

"Those chili dogs hit the spot," Mitch said patting his stomach as he rocked backward in his chair. "All I need is a slice of my Miss American's pie and it'll be a perfect day."

"Sorry. There isn't any pie," Walt said as the edge of his

mouth curled up ever so slightly.

"No pie?" Mitch sat forward and looked at his empty plate.

"What are your plans now that you're home from the war, Mitch?" Walt asked.

"I've got a job at a realty firm. Been doing a lot of office work, mostly. Hope to get my Realtor's license soon and start selling mansions in the Vestal Hills to all them wealthy foreign doctors." He glanced at Joachim, who just smirked in response. "Gonna build us a fortune, sugarplum," he said as he patted Elaina's head, "and one day that'll be us atop those Vestal Hills."

Elaina smiled brightly. Dee Dee leaned forward and rested her arms on the table.

"Tell us about your family. Do your parents live around here?"

"Divorced," he said, nodding at Walt, whose hand rolled into a fist under the table. "Dad lives in Horseheads and Mom lives in a mobile home park in Zephyrhills, Florida."

"Siblings?"

"Only child."

"Have any family around here?"

"I do now," Mitch responded with a sugar-eating grin. "Hey sugarplum, can you fetch me another beer?" He patted her head again.

"She's not a dog," Dee Dee muttered to Joachim as she rolled her eyes.

"What?" Mitch glared at her.

"Did you go to school around here?" Walt interrupted.

"No. I didn't grow up here."

"Where did you grow up?" Now Walt was leaning toward the table.

"A little town in the North Country by the St. Lawrence. You've never heard of it."

"Try me." Dee Dee stared at her brother-in-law as he leaned back in his chair with an air of nonchalance.

"Dee Dee, what's your *problem*?" Elaina frowned.

"Riverton."

Dee Dee shrugged her shoulders. Mitch laughed.

"Knew you wouldn't know it. Population 780. And that's not including the dogs." He snorted, and looked straight at Dee Dee.

"What's your connection to this area then?" Walt asked.

"A buddy of mine in the Navy went to Johnson City High School."

"What's his name," Dee Dee pressed. "Maybe we know him?"

"Hey!" Elaina snapped at her sister. "Take it easy on my husband." Mitch patted her head again and laughed.

"I ought to set you folks loose on al-Qaida. You'd do an ace job squeezing out intelligence secrets from them." He stood up and put out his hand toward Elaina.

"Hey, sugarplum, what do you say we go home and hit the hay?" Mitch winked toward Dee Dee and Joachim. "You newlyweds know what I'm talkin' about."

Dee Dee curled her fingers into the chair cushion. Could this guy be any more repulsive?

"Thanks for dinner, Pop. See you at the diner tomorrow. Dee Dee, will you guys still be here?"

"We've both gotta head back for classes so we're going to take off early." She stood up to give her sister a hug. "Love you, Sis." Dee Dee held her sister tight. "Give me a call if you ever need anything."

Mitch held out his arms to hug Dee Dee but she shook his hand instead. "Nice to meet you, Mitch."

The minute the two walked out the door, Joachim looked at Walt and Dee Dee.

"I don't trust him," he said.

"I don't either, son," Walt said as he pulled down the bottle of Irish whiskey from the cupboard. "Want some?" He held out the bottle. They nodded and sat in silence as they sipped. The only noise was the sound of the kitchen clock. It was ticking away like a time bomb.

~ Chapter 7 ~

Things soon changed.

The moment Rhey returned from his cruise he called the diner. Walt told him the news about Elaina and gave him her new number. Rhey was stunned. He detected sadness in Walt's voice as he recited the seven numbers scribbled on the notepad next to the phone. Ooh, this must be really bad, Rhey thought. Walt was such an easygoing guy. Most straight men acted nervous around Rhey; as if just by speaking with him they'd contract gayness. Not Walt. He treated Rhey like one of the guys, which Rhey found very refreshing.

Rhey rehearsed what he would say to Elaina. He had to make sure his tone was non-judgmental because the last thing he wanted to do was hurt Elaina's feelings. Should he tell her about the scarf, or wait 'til they got together at the diner? Now that she was married, would Elaina still be free for their Friday night picture shows?

He steeled himself and dialed her number. A man answered. Rhey was already nervous.

"Hi, may I speak with Elaina?" he asked, ready to extend pleasantries to her husband with his next words.

"She's not here. Who's *this*?" Mitch's military tone startled Rhey and he hung up. *Oh c'mon, I'm such a 'fraidy cat*, Rhey thought as he laughed to himself. He picked up the phone to try again, thinking he'd introduce himself and smooth over that unfortunate hang-up. His hand froze on the receiver. He was not getting a good vibe at the moment. The local psychic Jeremy Candor read his aura once and said he had clairvoyant ability. "Listen to the omens of danger you get," Candor said. Rhey slunk away from the phone and looked back at it as if it would explode suddenly. This was not the right time to call. He'd wait for Elaina to make the first move.

* * *

Shortly into their marriage, Elaina discovered Mitch couldn't boil water if he tried. At least that's the joke he made repeatedly to her as he watched her prepare his supper each night.

"I'm the breadwinner; you're the bread baker," he'd laugh. Truth was Elaina had started feeling like the *breadwinner*. She'd rise early to go off to the diner, pray that Mary Jo wasn't out for the drama du jour, come home as soon as she could, fix Mitch's dinner, clean the house and feign astonishment at his lovemaking ability. She was so tired all the time. She thought it must be easier to be the CEO of a Fortune 500 company.

Mitch didn't like simple meals such as pizza and salad. This quirk must have been related to his years in the service. He expected a square meal like he'd get in the mess hall, he'd say. And of course, there'd have to be pie. Fresh pie. Not pie brought home from the diner or any other leftover food. All his meals had to be prepared especially for him, Mitch said.

Here he was, a veteran who'd looked terrorists in the eye and never blinked (according to the stories he recalled), yet he was totally helpless in the kitchen. What does it take to broil a couple of hot dogs, dump a can of beans into a pot and rip open a bag of potato chips?

She was surprised about another aspect of Mitch's dining habits. For a man who had sailed around the world to every exotic locale you could imagine, his food palate was surprisingly limited. It was stuck in the comfort food range. Elaina wondered if other people in the armed services suffered from this culinary disability.

His naval training had instilled in Mitch a need for routine in his life. He got up the same time every day—after she was already at work. He'd swing by the diner for a cup of coffee and slice of apple pie on Saturday morning after working out at the gym. He even drank from the same coffee mug at home every day, despite the fact that one cupboard held more than twenty choices.

It was the same with the menu Elaina prepared for him at home. She was lucky that there were seven different menus he liked so she didn't have to repeat one during the week. They required little skill and even less imagination. Although she enjoyed baking the pies day after day at the diner, being boxed-in by this dull cooking routine bugged her.

One evening when she got home from work there was a note from Mitch saying he'd be a little late. He was joining his boss at a home in Vestal they were showing to a doctor from out of town. She was happy for the chance to relax a little bit and do something for herself.

"Hey Rhey, it's me. Sorry I haven't called sooner but this

newlywed business keeps me pretty busy."

"Hello Mrs. Johnson. It's nice to *finally* hear from you. So when can I come over and inspect your humble chateau?"

"I was thinking I'd ask Mitch if it would be all right if you came over on Sunday afternoon for a little while."

Rhey raised his eyebrow. "You have to ask permission?"

"Well, you know, Mitch is in the military. He has his routines. And if the slightest thing is disturbed he gets a little moody. I think it's post-traumatic stress."

"Sounds more like he's a spoiled brat. Oops. Did I say that?" Rhey laughed. "Anyway, I can't wait to give you your present from Greece, you know the one I've been holding onto for a month—*ahem*—and show you the pictures. Oh El, we've got to take a cruise to Greece together sometime. It will simply blow your mind."

"Don't know if Mitch would go for that now that he's back in civilian life. It's so funny—for all his world travels, he really is a homebody. Can't wait for you to meet him. You'll think he's quite a dish, despite his brattiness. Oh, there's Mitch's car in the driveway. Listen, gotta go. Love ya."

"Love you too, Elly," Rhey said to the dial tone. Why did she think Mitch would be invited on their cruise?

"Mmm, I smell pork chops. Must be Tuesday," Mitch said as he walked in their apartment.

"How did you know," Elaina feigned surprise as he kissed her neck.

"Well, you're just so dependable, sugarplum. If I come home and smell ham and scalloped potatoes, I know it's

Monday. If chicken's roasting, it's Sunday. Meat loaf means Wednesday. And if fish is fryin', it means...."

She'd stopped listening as soon as he called her dependable. Mitch held his hands out to her waiting for her response. Elaina could smell beer on his breath.

"I don't know, Mitch. You tell me."

"Sorry, I skipped a day. Must have confused you. If fish is fryin', it's...."

"Friday." She wiped her brow and checked on the pork chops in the oven.

Mitch reached into the refrigerator for a can of beer, popped it open and took a deep swig.

"Now on Saturday we have...."

"Hot dogs with piccalilli relish. Baked beans with three slices of smoked bacon on top. Macaroni salad made with that sandwich spread, not mayonnaise. And Wise potato chips." Elaina sounded as if she were giving an order to a waitress.

"That's my girl. Very good. Now what's my favorite meal of the week?" He sank the full weight of his body into the chair, sounding like a tractor trailer hitting a speed bump.

"Have you been drinking?"

"Yep. Dick Baburka and I stopped by the Glenmere for a couple brewskies after we showed the Patterson house. Why? Do you have a problem with that?"

"Wash up. Dinner is almost ready."

Mitch slammed the beer can on the table, shoved back the chair and went over to the sink.

"You didn't answer! What's my favorite meal?"

"I give up. Tell me."

"I can't believe you've forgotten what it is!"

She scooped mashed potatoes onto a platter then arranged the breaded pork chops around them. Just for something different, she scattered parsley sprigs over it all to finish the presentation, like she'd seen in that cooking magazine at Rhey's house.

"Did I *ask* for grass on my pork chops?" Mitch glowered.

She ignored him and set the platter on the table. When she put the warmed apple sauce into a serving bowl, she sprinkled some cinnamon on top. While her hand was still over the bowl with the shaker, Mitch grabbed it and stopped her.

"*What* are you doing?"

"I just wanted to spice things up a bit."

"Did you ask Mitch, your husband, if that's what he wanted, Elaina?"

"No," she said trying to pull her wrist away. "I just thought...."

"I told you," he yelled, "don't do *anything* without asking Mitch first!" He gripped her wrist tighter.

"Ow! You're hurting me!"

"Say yes."

"Yes what?" He twisted her wrist backward.

"Yes sir." She mumbled the answer he demanded and he released her hand.

"Good. Now serve me my dinner. By the way, it's creamed chipped beef on freedom fries. That's my favorite meal of the week. Thursdays. Don't forget." He slammed back into his seat and drained the can of beer in a loud gulp.

"Sugarplum," he said holding the empty can out, "fetch me another."

Elaina ate in silence. Sure he'd been moody before, but she'd never seen him explode like this. There must have been something really dark that he'd witnessed in the war, something still haunting him. Why else would he go from pleasant to surly so fast? How stupid she was to change the routine. She'd never try that again. Ugh, she had a couple loads of laundry to do tonight and housecleaning too. They were two other areas in his life where he was totally hopeless. At least he didn't mind putting away his own clothes. He was almost fanatical about folding them himself, another ingrained military habit she thought.

How did their daily menu fall into this routine so quickly? With her long days at the diner and answering Mitch's every need at home, she had no time to herself to analyze what had been happening.

That night as she washed the dishes, she looked out the window at the sunset. He'd called her dependable. That sounded as unromantic as a beached Susquehanna carp baking in the sun. She was now in the same category as a John Deere tractor or a Sears Diehard battery. Dependable, she hissed. Their apartment was small, thankfully, so it didn't take her long to finish cleaning up after her laundry was done and folded. Mitch spent the evening watching a Yankees game on TV. Watching sports was another one of his needs.

She kept thinking about what he said, and the next

morning when she was rolling out pie dough she asked her father about it.

"Pop, would you call me dependable?"

Walt smiled.

"Well, you're no Mary Jo, who by the way called in sick again."

"No! You're *kidding* me." Elaina stopped what she was doing and sighed as her shoulders slumped from the weight of all the work to come.

"This time it's her youngest she has to take care of. Has the 24-hour bug."

"You'll never fire her, will ya, Pop? 'Cause you know you can always depend on me to be here."

"No, I won't be firing her because I think or *don't* think you're dependable. We're family here at the diner. You've gotta give and take with family. Mary Jo's just the needy child in the bunch."

Elaina was grateful that it was Wednesday, meat loaf night. It was one of the easiest menus to prepare for Mitch. By the time she'd get home she'd be exhausted from all her baking and waitressing for Mary Jo.

"What's wrong with being dependable, anyway? I think it's a commendable quality," Walt said. Elaina brushed her brow with the back of her floured hand.

"Oh, it's just something Mitch said. I'm being overly sensitive, I guess."

Walt smiled at his daughter.

"I'd take a dependable wife any day over some woman

who looks like a movie star."

It was another one of his awkward compliments, and she knew what her father meant. His words still stung her. Ugly. Dependable. Wasn't that what she was trying to overcome by running away with Mitch?

By the end of the day she was exhausted. She kissed her father goodnight and rushed home to prepare dinner for Mitch. The meat loaf was nearly done baking and she was mashing potatoes when the phone rang.

"Sugarplum, I'm gonna be a little late tonight. Dick and I have to go over some paperwork for a closing tomorrow morning."

She stood there, masher in one hand, frowning at the phone. Reheated mashed potatoes are just not the same, she thought.

"How long will you be?"

She heard his boss snicker in the background. Mitch must have put her on the speaker phone.

"Soon enough."

"Well, don't stay too long at the Glenmere. Be careful not to spill any beer on your *paperwork*."

There was a pause at the other end and it sounded like he'd switched off the speaker phone and was cupping the receiver so Dick couldn't hear.

"You know what, Elaina? I had a big surprise for you tonight. I'm going to get a big bonus for helping Dick sell this property. I thought maybe we'd go away for a mini-vacation this weekend, maybe go someplace in the Poconos. You know, to one of them places with the heart-shaped tubs? But now you've just gone and ruined that, haven't you. *Haven't you?*"

"I'm sorry. I'm just so tired from work. Mary Jo called in sick again today. I had to do all her work and mine today. I've just made a beautiful dinner for you. Now it will be cold."

"Hear that, Elaina? *Do* you? That's the world's smallest violin playing the world's saddest song. You think *I* didn't get tired on that aircraft carrier, day after day guiding jets in safely after their sorties? Do you know what type of pressure that is? If a jet misses it could crash into the ocean. Or it could hit the deck and explode and burn you and many of the crew alive. And do you know how hot it is standing on a flight deck in the middle of the Persian Gulf with the sun beating down on you and you're breathing in jet fuel fumes all day? Oh, but I guess putting your *life* on the line every day can't compare with the difficulties of being a pie maker at a diner or the technical skills needed to be a waitress."

"I'll see you when you get home then," Elaina said shaking. There it was again. That cold military quality to Mitch's voice scared her. She hung up the phone and wiped the tears streaming down her face.

* * *

The next day, Rhey stopped in at the diner during her break time.

"I got tired of waiting for your phone call inviting me over on the weekend, Mrs. Johnson. I decided to stop by and see if you could spare a few moments of your time." She blushed and pointed toward the door.

"Let's go sit at the picnic table."

It was good to be outside breathing in fresh air. The warm sun felt like the hands of a masseuse on her back and the breeze carried the softest scent of balsam.

Rhey set a box tied with a pretty blue bow on the table. "For you, Elly. It's from Santorini." Rhey watched with his hands folded like he was praying as she opened the gift bag. She pulled out a long scarf in a shade of blue that matched the color of the Aegean. The ends were trimmed with strands of sparkling beads—the longest one finished with a bead that looked like a blue eye.

"You see these beads everywhere in Greece. It's supposed to ward off evil," Rhey said pointing to the bead. "Here let me show you how they wear it." As he draped and adjusted the scarf he apologized for not buying her one in Monte Carlo as promised. He'd been a bit seasick that day and didn't go ashore. As she sat back, Rhey noticed the tiny diamond in her ring and cringed slightly.

"This scarf is so beautiful," Elaina said as she reached out to kiss him. "It means so much to me coming from you, my dear friend." A tear rolled across her cheek and she brushed it away.

"Of course it's beautiful. My taste is exquisite, as always. But I didn't mean for it to upset you. You were counting on the Monte Carlo scarf, is that it? I'm sorry, Elly. Maybe I can get you one online."

"No, that's not it. It's probably just my period. I've been so emotional lately. So tired."

Hmm, Rhey thought. He knew that her marriage would affect her, but it shouldn't be in this way. She was not her cheery self.

"Hey, Elaina, come sneak away to the gallery tomorrow night. Just like old times. I'll show you pictures of the Greek gods I met." He made her laugh briefly, but then her thoughts turned to Mitch. She'd have to have his dinner ready and then make up a lie so she could go to Rhey's. Was there a way she could do it safely? After he came home late last night, maybe he'd be late again Friday. She couldn't count on it though.

"Um, another time, Rhey. Mitch has been working late 'til all different times lately, and he really counts on dinner being ready when he arrives."

"Speaking of," Rhey seized the change in subject to address the marriage. "How's the wedded bliss these days? Has he shocked and awed you in the bedroom? Oh El, I can't believe I just said something so *tawdry*."

Elaina played with the blue eye bead on the scarf.

"It's fine. He's very affectionate."

"Fine? Affectionate? The man's got a porn star name and that's all you can say about his performance?"

"Um, well, he's my first...I guess everything is going OK."

"Hon, I'm not surprised about the virginity part," he said touching her arm. "I am about the other, though. I'd think you'd know if he were rocking your world."

"Well at first it was definitely like that. I'd certainly never been kissed like *that* before. But I'm just so tired all the time, Rhey, and he says he *has* to, you know, have it *every* night. He keeps saying that he has needs."

"And what about *your* needs? Ever think of saying: 'Sorry, I need a break so I'm going to my friend's gallery tonight to discuss other things in life just as important—such as art and beauty.' Or, is he a culture-phobe?"

"I could *never* say no."

"Why?" The fear on her face concerned Rhey.

"Because...he...I'm a...uh, I've gotta get back to work, Rhey."

"Friday night. The gallery. *Be* there!"

"I'll try," she said. "I just *love* this scarf."

Walt was talking to a customer at the counter when she walked in.

"If you need to have that oil leak looked at Dan, why not go across the street? We take our cars to Zahir all the time. He's a wonderful mechanic and honest, too. Won't do any unnecessary work just to jack up the bill."

"Zahir? What kind of a name is that?"

"American. He's *American*, for God's sake," Walt snapped at the man.

"I wouldn't take my car anywhere else," Elaina said as she put her apron back on. After paying his check, Dan did heed their advice and drove his car across the street.

A few hours later the diner was almost empty. Elaina went out back to the kitchen to start cleaning things up. Walt noticed she was not her talkative self.

"So, when should we plan the party for you and Dee Dee?"

"I dunno, Pop. I guess it depends on when Dee Dee and

Joachim can come to town. We're not going anywhere."

Walt turned around and looked at Elaina.

"Everything OK with you and Mitch?"

"Yeah, we're fine." She walked out of the kitchen quickly.

Zahir came in just as she was heading out the door for home.

"Any apple pie today?" he asked shyly.

"Sure. Pop, can you get a slice of the apple for Zahir?"

"Thanks for that customer you sent me today, Walt." Zahir called to him.

"How's business?" Walt said as he returned.

Zahir laughed nervously. "Oh, it could be better. Our regular customers are spreading the word about us. Slowly." He took out his wallet to pay.

"Put that away, son. You're money is no good here." Walt winked at him.

"Thank you very much. You people are always so kind. I am very blessed to know you both."

"Good neighbors like you aren't easy to find," Walt said as he wrapped up the pie.

Zahir held the door open for Elaina.

"That scarf you're wearing is beautiful. The blue is so, so...bright. It reminds me of sunshine on the ocean."

"Rhey brought it from Greece for me."

Zahir looked away as if he were trying to get the courage to say something to her.

"Did you know I got married, Zahir?" He looked back at her with the expression of a lost child, she thought.

"Yes. I heard congratulations are in order. I wish you much happiness." His face bore no happiness to correspond with what he said.

* * *

Mitch was waiting for Elaina when she got home.

"I'll start dinner right away," she said.

"Good. I'm starving, sugarplum. What's that thing around your neck?"

"A gift from my friend Rhey. He brought it back from Greece for me."

"I think it looks stupid, like you're a gypsy or something. Why don't you take it off?" He opened the refrigerator and pulled out a can of beer. "Seriously," he said popping the tab as he looked at her. "It makes you look like an A-rab."

Elaina ran her fingers over the evil eye bead.

"Who's this guy think he is, anyway, bringing my wife clothes?"

"He's been a good friend to me. I've known him longer than you."

"What's that supposed to mean? Just because some flaming gallery owner tosses you a cheap scarf, you run around all full of yourself. It doesn't look good for a patriot like me to have my wife hanging around such people."

"Such *people*—what's that supposed to mean, Mitch? How dare you say that about...."

Mitch slammed his beer on the table, stood up and blocked Elaina in by the stove.

"You know what they do to people in the military who sass

back? They discipline them!" He raised his hand toward her face and bared his teeth like a rabid dog.

She lowered her head and looked away, in anticipation of the impact of his hand on her face. Thankfully, he restrained himself.

"I don't want you hanging around that homo. Do you *understand*? Now cook my dinner, Elaina! Dammit! Here it is my favorite meal of the week and you're spoiling it for me." Mitch pushed his chair into the table, grabbed his beer and went out on the couch to watch TV. Elaina unwrapped the scarf from her neck carefully, folded it up and stashed it in a kitchen drawer.

She was too afraid to cry aloud. With her back to him, she allowed tears to roll down her cheeks silently without brushing them away. She could taste the salt in them as they passed over her lips. Even the slightest whimper, she feared, would bring his hand across her face.

Elaina melted butter in the saucepan and then added the flour, stirring constantly to make a paste. Then she added hot milk, whisking back and forth to make it smooth. When the sauce thickened, she stirred in the chipped beef and seasoned it with fresh ground pepper. The french fries were browning in the hot oven as she cooked frozen peas in another pot. He could smell that supper was almost ready, and parked himself back in his seat at the table. She spread the french fries on a platter, then poured the chipped beef over the top and set it on the table. Mitch had already started eating when she brought over the bowl of buttered peas.

"Thanks, sugarplum. What are you havin'?" He laughed as he mocked hoarding the platter to himself. She held the saucepan under the faucet and filled it up halfway with water to ease the cleanup after dinner. Before she sat down, the phone rang.

"Hey Sis, how are you?" Dee Dee said.

"Hi! Great to hear from you. What a nice surprise."

"Who is it?" Mitch said loudly.

"It's Dee Dee."

"Well, it's been a while and I haven't heard from you. Just calling to see how you and Pop and Mitch, of course, all are."

"Tell her we just sat down to dinner," he bellowed so loud that Dee Dee could hear him over the phone. His tone alarmed her.

"Everything OK down there, Sis?"

"Yeah, fine. You were saying?"

"I was wondering if...."

"Tell her to hang up and call back. Come eat your dinner, Elaina!"

"Sounds like I called at a bad time."

Elaina's heart sank. She wanted to talk with Dee Dee so badly, but was afraid of what might happen if she rattled Mitch further.

"Um, can I call you back later, Sis? I'm sorry."

"No problem. Bye." Dee Dee hung up and shook her head.

"That was a short conversation," Joachim said.

"Poor Elaina. That Mitch is such a jerk. He was screaming at her in the background because their dinner was on the table and he was hungry. What an asshole!"

"That's alarming. Should we be concerned for her safety?"

"I definitely am. I better call Pop and let him know what's going on. Chances are Elaina hasn't told him a thing about this."

* * *

Friday morning Mary Jo called the diner to say her car was in the shop because they hit a deer Thursday night on the Vestal Parkway. Another day of doing two jobs, Elaina thought. Ugh.

"Pop, you've got to talk with Mary Jo. I'm beat. This is getting ridiculous. Last night Mitch was cranky that I was a little late for making his dinner." Walt was sharpening his carving knife as she spoke. An image flashed in his mind of it plunging into Mitch's chest. Good Lord, he thought, what's becoming of me?

Later that morning the phone rang and Elaina answered saying, "The Terminal Diner, may I help you?"

Although the family had often joked about the name Walt inherited for their diner, to hear Elaina say it aloud that morning chilled Dee Dee.

"Sis, you never returned my call last night. I was wondering if you were OK."

"I'm fine. Sorry I couldn't speak with you longer last night but I was a little late getting home and preparing Mitch's dinner so he was kinda cranky."

"So I heard in the background. Why didn't you call me back later?"

"Well, I had to do the dishes and the laundry and pick up the house. Then Mitch said it was time for bed."

"Oh, so he tells you when it's time for bed now?" Dee Dee tapped a pen loudly on the notebook in front of her.

"Well, um, it's not that. It's, you know, his needs."

"His *needs*?" Dee Dee was afraid of what would come out of her mouth next, and bit her hand to control herself.

Elaina looked around to see if anyone was within earshot, then lowered her voice. "As he says every day, he's a man in his prime and he needs fulfillment. For his health. He wants it every night, Sis. I'm so tired."

"God, Elaina. Are you on birth control?" Dee Dee feared a mini-Mitch might already be on the way.

"Yeah. I didn't want to—I want kids so bad it's killing me—but he insisted that I go on the pill right away. You know, in case he gets redeployed soon. Mitch said we should also wait until we can afford a place of our own and have the space to raise a family."

Translation: until he finds someone better, Dee Dee thought.

"Anyway, Dad wanted to nail down a date for our party. I was thinking the second weekend in September. Would that work?"

"I'll ask Mitch. Listen, I'm filling in for Mary Jo again and the lunch crowd is coming in."

"She's out again? That woman has more drama than a Shakespeare festival."

"Hah! Man, you can say that again. OK, I'll talk with you

later. Love you, Dee Dee."

Elaina's back had been to the door, so she didn't see Simon come in. When she turned around and saw him in the back booth, he waved at her. She thought about calling Rhey. Then she remembered what Mitch said about him the night before.

"Hi Simon," she said filling up his mug with hot water. "Haven't seen you in weeks. How have you been?"

"Busy." He saw the wedding band on her finger.

"Looks like you've been busy, too."

She blushed as she handed him a menu. "Yeah, I ran off and got married."

Simon nodded and put a sachet of tea in the mug.

"You know, I've been thinking about those beautiful sculptures that you make. I showed them to my friend Rhey, he owns the gallery down the road. He thought they were very good and would like to hold a show featuring your work. Said he didn't know of any other artists working in the aluminum foil medium."

"The old drive-in? I pass that every day."

"That's the place."

"How many would he need?"

"I dunno. I'd guess somewhere between 20 to 30 pieces?"

"I'll take a box of them over and he can decide what he needs. Each one tells a story. I'll let him figure it out."

"Great. Rhey will be thrilled. Do you have a phone number where he can contact you?"

Simon looked at the menu and didn't reply. She waited

and after an awkward silence walked back to the counter.

"I'll have the special," he called out to her.

When Simon left that day, she was disappointed that he didn't leave another sculpture behind. Instead she discovered a Sacajawea dollar coin tucked under the plate his sandwich had been on. There was also a small river stone with the underlined word "Sharon" written on it next to the coin. Elaina just shook her head and wondered if she'd ever understand his mysterious ways.

"Rhey," Elaina said on the phone. "Good news."

"You're coming over for a slideshow tonight?"

"No. Better news. Simon was just here and he agreed to do a show at your gallery."

"Wonderful. Why didn't you call me to let me know he was there?"

She ignored the question. "He said he'll bring by a box of the sculptures and let you connect the story they tell."

"Did he say when he'd stop by?"

"No. I asked for his phone number and he wouldn't answer. I didn't want to push it."

"Well I guess I'll see him when I see him. So, when are you arriving tonight?"

"Um...can't do it tonight."

"Why?"

"I have to make dinner for Mitch and he's not sure when he's going to be home."

"You never get a night off?"

It finally hit Elaina and she began to sob.

"Elly, what's the matter?"

"I'm sorry."

"For what? Why are you crying? Listen, I'm coming up there."

"No! Don't! You can't...."

"I can't what? Explain, please."

"If Mitch found out he'd...."

"Wait a minute. Did he tell you to stay away from me?"

"It was the scarf. He was jealous that you got it for me and...," she sobbed louder. Walt heard her crying and signaled to Angie to go over and see what was wrong. She ran over with a box of tissues.

"You OK, hon?"

Elaina nodded. "Rhey, I have to go. I'll call you again."

"Take care, Elly. Don't let that jerk get you down."

Angie daubed the tears off Elaina's face.

"Man trouble, hon?"

She nodded.

"Listen, my daddy taught us one thing—you can take the man out of the military but never the military out of the man. Takes them a while to adjust to real life again, that's all."

Elaina pouted and nodded again. "It sure does."

That night Rhey decided to set up a slideshow, just in case Elaina made a break for it and came over. The doorbell rang and he pumped his fist into the air. "Yay, she did it!" He poured a daiquiri, tossed in a paper umbrella and carried it over to the entrance to greet her. When he unlocked the door and opened it, he was surprised to see a tall man with a ponytail holding a large box instead.

"These are for the exhibit," Simon said.

"Oh, you must be Simon. Come in, come in. Let me just say, I'm a fan. Your work is fascinating. Tell me about it."

"I told Elaina that you can connect the stories they tell." He set the box down on the floor and looked around the gallery at the portraits by Rhey on display.

"This your work?" he said as he walked up close to a painting of a man who posed for Rhey on Santorini.

"Yes. I love working in oils."

"Hmm, nice technique. Painterly."

"Tell me, Simon, how do you get the detail in your sculptures? Why aluminum foil? It must be a difficult medium."

"Recycling," Simon said as he reached into his pocket and pulled out individually wrapped toothpicks, like the type by the cash register at The Terminal Diner. "I sculpt with these." Rhey's eyes widened at the thought that such beautiful art was created with simple kitchen items.

"Cinnamon-flavored." Simon held the sculpture out for Rhey to smell it. "We use cinnamon to cure snakebites." Rhey nodded at Simon as he wondered if this strange artist was mocking him some way.

"How much should we ask for your pieces? I get a twenty-five percent commission on all sales."

"You decide. When will the exhibit be?"

"The pastel artist I had booked for September just canceled. Would that be OK?"

"I'll come by September 30th to pick them up." He walked out of the gallery without saying goodbye.

Rhey carried the box into his apartment and scattered the sculptures on his kitchen table.

"Great. Where do I start to connect the stories? I'm gonna need more daiquiris." He wished Elaina would show up but at this hour it seemed unlikely. He missed her company so much. They were such a perfect faux couple.

He stirred the umbrella in his drink, looked at the heap of tiny aluminum sculptures, and went off to watch his slideshow instead.

~ Chapter 8 ~

Something wasn't right.

Zahir was driving his tow truck up Airport Road on Saturday morning when he saw a car ahead drifting into the left lane. He tapped his car horn to alert the driver and the person reacted and drifted back into the right lane. The closer he got, he realized it was Elaina's car. He could see her behind the wheel. She started veering left again and he beeped the car louder and she over-corrected, almost going off the road.

What's the matter with her, he wondered. She couldn't be drunk at this hour. (Not that he thought she was the type to ever get drunk.) Was she on some medication that was making her drowsy? He followed her into the diner's parking lot.

She yawned as she got out of the car. Zahir thought she looked pale and too thin. When he got up close to her, he noticed purplish circles under her eyes. He'd never seen her looking so run down.

"Good morning, Elaina. Are you OK? You were drifting all over the road back there."

She yawned as she nodded.

"I'm just so tired, Zahir."

"Late night?"

She turned away from him and he saw a black-and-blue mark on the side of her face.

"Elaina, you're injured!" He thought maybe she'd suffered a concussion somehow and that's why she was having trouble steering her car.

"Oh yeah, that. Um, I fell in the kitchen last night." As she put the key in the door, Zahir saw more black and blues on her wrist.

"You hit your wrist, too?"

"Don't worry, Zahir. I'm OK. Thank you so much for checking. Stop by for a piece of pie later."

"I will, Elaina. Have a good day."

Walt found Elaina sleeping in a booth when he arrived. It was obvious she hadn't started baking yet. He wondered if she'd spent the night there.

"Poor thing needs her rest," he said as he filled the coffee pot. He preheated the oven, took the muffin batter out of the refrigerator and filled the tins. He also pulled out some reserve pies from the freezer and put them all in the oven when it was ready.

The aromas of coffee brewing and baking desserts roused Elaina from her slumber. She walked groggily into the kitchen and yawned at her father. He noticed the black and blues immediately.

"Elaina! What *happened* to you?"

She yawned as she tied her apron.

"I slipped on a greasy floor in the kitchen last night while cooking Mitch's fish fry. He didn't get home until ten. I was really tired and wasn't being careful. The oil got too hot and splattered all over." She peeked into the oven.

"Did you make these pies, Pop?"

"No, they're some of your reserves. We won't be open for a while. Why don't you go get some more sleep in the booth and I'll wake you when it's time to open."

She yawned again and gave her father a hug before she lay down. It wasn't long before she was sound asleep.

Walt watched her as he thought about those marks on her face and wrist. He knew they weren't from any accident. It looked like a strong hand had grabbed her wrist; the black-and-blue marks lined up like the imprint of fingers. He cringed as he thought the marks were probably made by Mitch. *Bastard.*

How could he free his daughter from her bad marriage? Could he pay Mitch to leave? Could he hide her somewhere out West with Maria? He still had her phone number someplace. It broke his heart to think that anyone would hurt his firstborn. She looked as vulnerable to him this moment as when Maria first handed her to him in the hospital. He recalled how perfect she was as he wrapped his arms around her tiny body. Cute as a button nose. Perfect long fingers that even had fingernails. It sounds stupid, but that simple detail amazed him. Now her hands were knobby and red from years of hard work for him. Had he somehow failed in his promise made the day she was born to protect his precious daughter from harm? He wiped the tears away with the back of his hand. If he ever caught Mitch striking Elaina, Walt would make sure he didn't live to see the next dawn.

Walt wondered what Elaina's life would have been like if

Maria had stayed. She'd have had a chance to go to college probably, maybe meet a decent young man with plenty of dreams they could share. He wasn't the type to hold grudges, but Walt did blame Maria partly for the mess their daughter was in now. Maybe she should be told what's going on. He didn't think he could muster up the courage to call Maria, though. The wound from her desertion was still festering inside Walt. He started thinking about the man who spirited her away. Was he a bully like Mitch? As hurt as Walt still was, he hoped that wasn't the case for his ex-wife. No woman deserved to be treated like this.

"A penny for your thoughts, Walt." He turned around and saw Angie smiling at him. "You were just a world away right then, weren't you?"

"Hah, you know me too well, Angie. Hey, would you do me a favor and wake up sleepyhead in the last booth. She had a rough time last night."

Angie looked toward Elaina and sighed. "There's nothin' good about that sailor she married, is there hon?" Walt shrugged his shoulders. Angie hated to see him looking so sad. He was the kindest, best boss she'd ever had. He didn't deserve this grief.

"You a bettin' man, Walt?" she asked, a mischievous look on her face.

"Sometimes. When the odds are in my favor and after I've tapped the lucky pound note."

"Well, I bet you that it wasn't Mitch who paid my dental bill." Walt guffawed.

"I suspect the person has something to do with this diner."

"That so?" Walt raised an eyebrow as he walked back into the kitchen.

"I think it's that state trooper who comes in Saturday morning. You know, the cute young thing."

Walt grinned as he scraped hash across the griddle.

* * *

Zahir was changing the oil on a car when Malik called out to him.

"It's Ahmed on the phone for you."

Zahir wiped the oil off his hands and picked up the phone inside American's car sales office.

"I'm having trouble locating that sailor you asked me about," Ahmed said. "There doesn't appear to be any Mitch Johnson who has served in Operations Iraqi Freedom or Enduring Freedom. No record of any hero at the Pentagon on 9/11 by that name, either. I found a Mateo Johnson from Chula Vista, California, who served most recently but he's only 19. That's the closest I could find. Do you think this guy is lying?"

Zahir put his hand over his mouth. Poor Elaina.

"Either this guy was involved in some deep cover Special Ops or his story is completely false."

"Thank you, Ahmed. This will help us. Please say hello to the family for me." Zahir hung up the phone as images of Elaina's black and blues flashed in his mind. He could feel anger rising in him as his hand clenched a wrench. He looked out the garage window toward the diner. Walt must be told. It would be easier to do that than tell Elaina. He couldn't bear to see her in any more pain.

Later that day, after the lunch hour crowd left, Zahir decided to stop by for the piece of pie Elaina promised him. He took off his coveralls, washed up and walked across the road. Elaina was sitting on a stool, her chin resting on her arms folded across the counter.

"Hey, no sleeping on the job," he said, tapping her on the shoulder.

Her eyes brightened and she smiled when she turned around and saw him.

"I promised you some pie, didn't I?" She rose slowly from the stool, disappeared into the kitchen and returned after a few minutes with a slice of peanut butter fluff. "Thanks so much for watching over me this morning. You truly are my angel." She handed him a fork and napkin. "I'm sorry, we're out of apple. I hope you like peanut butter."

"If you made it, I know it's delicious, Elaina. Are you on your break?"

"Nah. I'm under Pop's orders to take it easy. He says my mom was prone to anemia when she was my age and he doesn't want me to wear myself out."

Mitch and his boss Dick Baburka drove into the parking lot just as Zahir and Elaina were talking. He saw her legs dangling like a schoolgirl's on the stool next to that Arab and she was laughing and playing with her hair. Zahir must have said something funny, and Mitch saw her touch his arm playfully as she laughed. Here he had brought Dick over to meet his wife and she was flirting with that Arab grease monkey. Mitch was furious.

When he walked in the door, Elaina stood up immediately and moved away from Zahir. She'd been so tired, she'd let her guard down and thought the diner was a haven from him.

"Hey, sugarplum," Mitch said giving her a kiss. Zahir noticed Elaina's whole body stiffen when Mitch touched her. "I was just in the neighborhood and wanted you to meet my boss, Dick Baburka. Dick, this is the wife."

As he shook her hand, Elaina could see him staring at her black and blues.

"Elaina's a bit of a klutz," Mitch said. "Slipped on the floor last night when she was cooking my fish fry. Didn't you, hon?"

She let go of Dick's hand and turned away quickly, so he wouldn't see the anger on her face. Zahir tightened his grip on his fork as he ate the slice of pie.

"Dick's coming over for dinner tonight, so I was wondering if you could make Sunday night's dinner tonight and we'll have hot dogs tomorrow."

"Roast chicken?" Elaina asked, the volume of her voice lowered by the fear of making any statement that might set her husband off. "But that means I'll have to go to the grocery and start dinner early."

"Dick and I will have ourselves a little happy hour at the Glenmere and we'll give you a call from there to see if everything's ready. Oh, and sugarplum, don't forget to make a fresh pie. I've been bragging on you to Dick about your apple pie. Told him how I call you my Miss American Pie." Mitch started laughing out loud and patted Zahir on the back. "'Cause you know how much I love everything *American*."

Zahir gripped the fork harder and imagined himself spinning around on the stool and plunging it into Mitch's chest.

"See you later, sugarplum." She cringed at hearing the sickening way Mitch used that nickname.

As soon as Dick and Mitch drove away, Elaina slipped off her apron.

"I've gotta go, Pop. I have to shop, get a pie baked, and roast a chicken...."

"Take an apple pie from the freezer. He'll never know."

"You think I could get away with that?"

"Sure. Ply him with beer and he won't taste the difference. Go on...we'll hold down the fort here."

"Thank you for the pie." Zahir smiled at her. "You're not just a pie maker, you're an artist. I think I might like this one better than the apple." Elaina grinned and leaned forward to give him a quick kiss on his cheek then dashed out the door.

Zahir touched his face where she'd kissed him. It felt warm, and the scent of lemony dish detergent on her lingered in the air. He inhaled deeply. It could have been the most precious perfume in all of Arabia.

Walt came out with an order of cheeseburgers and fries for customers in a booth and Zahir tried to pay him for the pie.

"Get out of here. You're money's still no good here," Walt said to him out of the corner of his mouth.

Zahir took a couple steps toward the door then looked back at him.

"Walt...there's something I must tell you about Mitch."

"I know, Zahir," Walt said as he stood next to the door. "She didn't fall. You can tell when a bruise is caused by the hand of a coward."

"I agree. But there is *more* I have to tell you. Stop by the garage tonight. After work."

"You've got it, son."

The news of Mitch lying about his military service didn't surprise Walt. He'd already noticed that his son-in-law spoke in broad terms about his service in the Navy. There were never any details offered by him, such as the name of a commanding officer. Walt hoped that perhaps he was actually involved in some sort of ultra-secret Special Ops work, but his gut told him otherwise. If what Zahir found out was true, what an insult it was to the brave men and women actually putting their lives on the line for this country. There was not a thing Walt found redeeming about Mitch's character.

"So who do you suppose he *really* is, Zahir?"

"I don't know. How are we going to let Elaina know?"

"I don't think we should say anything yet. Mitch might harm her more if he senses she's on to him. I've got some friends in the Sheriff's Department. We'll have a little chat and see what the options are."

"If I can be of help in any way...."

"You've already been a tremendous help, Zahir. I wish to God she was married to someone like you, instead." Walt gave Zahir a bear hug. "You feel more like a son to me than Mitch does. How's business? Picking up?"

"Actually, yes. It helps to have the best diner in town across the road."

The frozen pie was baked. Elaina had to pull the chicken out of the oven or else it would burn. Gravy congealed in a pot on the stove. The mashed potatoes were already cold.

Elaina was exhausted. She just wanted to crawl into bed and hide under the covers. She couldn't though, for fear she'd be in a deep sleep when Mitch and Dick showed up. And if Mitch found her that way, there'd be bigger hell to pay than last night's.

She was nodding off in a chair at the kitchen table when the two men stumbled in.

"Sugarplum? We're here for our dinner."

Elaina sprung from the chair, turned the oven back on and stirred the gravy as they came into the kitchen.

"Everything's ready. I just have to warm it back up." Mitch stared at her.

"Why don't you fellas sit down and help yourself to a beer. It'll just be a couple minutes." She hoped her father's advice would work. Maybe if Mitch was drunk enough, she wouldn't have to fulfill "his needs" later on, as well. It'd be the first decent night's sleep she'd gotten since their honeymoon.

She bustled around the kitchen as they yammered on about real estate gossip. Dick belched and Mitch slapped his back.

"Hah! Good one there, Dick."

Within fifteen minutes she had the dinner on the table. Just as she was sitting down the phone rang. Mitch frowned.

"I'll get it," he said yanking the receiver off the phone. "Yeah? She's here, Walt, but I'm just sitting down to my dinner. She'll call you later." He slammed the phone down.

"You just hung up on my dad?"

Mitch picked up his knife and gritted his teeth in a terrifying manner that reminded her of Jack Nicholson in that movie "The Shining."

"We have company, Elaina. It's impolite. You've got to talk with your family about calling during my dinnertime."

"But you never come home at the same time. How are they to know?"

He gave her that look again. She didn't say another word. Instead she ate her meal silently as Dick and Mitch tried to one-up each other with off-color jokes.

"How 'bout that barmaid Kirsten at the Glenmere," Mitch said with a leer. Elaina could see him checking her response from the corner of his eye. She kept her face expressionless.

"I'd like to pull her taps." Dick smirked. The two guffawed and while doing so, Dick accidentally spit out a little bit of mashed potato onto Elaina's plate. She was repulsed instantly and felt like she might gag. Could his boss be any viler?

She cleared the dinner plates and flicked on the coffee maker. While Mitch was distracted by another dumb joke of Dick's, she had made sure the coffee was decaf. No sense in destroying the beer buzz they had going. Apple pie warmed in the oven as she worked.

"That pie sure smells delicious, sugarplum." Please God, she prayed in silence. Don't let him notice it isn't fresh-made.

"Would you like your pie a la mode?" She asked Dick. He looked right at her breasts and sniggered.

"Sure, hon, I'll take whatever you're offering tonight." He licked his lips. She cringed. I need a shower, she thought.

As the men ate their pie, Elaina walked into the living room and plopped on the couch. She thought maybe she could rest there for a few minutes until it was time to clean up the kitchen. Her back ached and her feet were swollen. She sank blissfully into the overstuffed couch. Just a couple of minutes there would recharge her.

Sunlight warmed her face. Elaina bolted upright and glanced around the room. Ohmigod, she thought, did I spend the night on the couch? Her watch said 10 a.m. She grinned as she tiptoed toward the bedroom, thinking her father gave her good advice about the beer. If she could just slip under the covers without Mitch waking up, all would be OK.

The bed was still made and it was obvious Mitch hadn't slept there. She ran to the front door and peeked out the window. Dick's car was gone and so was Mitch's motorcycle. Where were they? There were no notes on the kitchen table that was still covered with dessert dishes and coffee cups. The answering machine's light wasn't blinking.

She went back to the couch and sat there frozen with her newfound freedom. Was Mitch just out for a cup of coffee somewhere with Dick? Had he left her? She didn't know what to do. Elaina went into the kitchen and cleaned up the rest of the dishes. That didn't take long. She thought about calling Pop or Dee Dee. Or Rhey. Was it too early? What would happen if Mitch returned and found her chatting on the phone, though?

She showered, dried her hair, tidied the living room and sat back on the couch. Should she be worried or relieved? Elaina turned on the TV to see if there was any news about an accident or two drunks arrested. It was Sunday morning though. There was no local news on. She switched TV channels mindlessly. It was the first time she'd been able to use the remote control since she moved in. Mitch was the designated channel surfer in their household.

A glorious morning beckoned her. She laced up her sneakers and strolled outside where a soft warm breeze caressed her face. At the far end of the apartment complex she saw a trail that led into nearby woods. She followed the path under a canopy of rustling Scotch pine branches and dappled sunlight. A cardinal sang *"birdee, birdee, birdee, birdee"* from one bough then flew in front of her flashing its crimson wings. The breeze carried the spicy clove-like scent of dame's rocket blooming on one side of the path. Elaina picked a small bouquet and inhaled its perfume as she continued on. There was a break in the trees up ahead where a small bridge crossed a gentle brook. She stood in the center of the bridge, arms folded as she listened to the softly gurgling water. With eyes closed she stood and exhaled all the tension out of her. Somehow she'd discovered a mental and spiritual oasis, as if crossing the bridge opened the door to another dimension. In the beauty of this calm setting, with the sound of water easing over mossy slate rocks, she was overcome with gratefulness to escape from her nightmare, even if it was for just a few minutes.

Her peace didn't last long. A tear slid down her cheek as her thoughts returned once more to Mitch and his whereabouts. She'd better get back in case he'd returned. Elaina peeked into the carport across the parking lot and was relieved to still see just her car out front and not his motorcycle. She unlocked the front door and daydreamed about what else she'd do with this sudden free time. That lasted a few seconds. Mitch was hiding right inside the door, and she tripped over his outstretched leg when she walked in.

"We better have a doctor examine you about this clumsiness of yours."

Elaina touched a brush burn on her elbow caused by sliding hard across the carpet with such dead weight.

"Where have you been?" He bellowed as he towered over her.

"I was looking for you. You weren't here when I woke up."

Mitch looked at the bouquet she'd been holding strewn across the floor.

"Yeah, I can see you were lookin' real hard, too. So hard you stopped to pick daisies along the way." He used his heel to grind them into the rug. "You're going to have to clean up this mess now."

"They aren't daisies." She had no idea why she said it. Why didn't I just keep my mouth shut, she thought.

"Are you correcting me? Who do you think you *are* correcting me—a patriot!"

"Honey," she said as she curled upright and folded her arms around her legs. "I think maybe you should go see someone about your post-traumatic stress. I know this isn't you talking. Remember Niagara Falls? Remember the good times we had on our honeymoon?"

Mitch snorted. "You think you know me, but you have no clue. Do you know how much you embarrassed me last night when I brought my boss over here and his dinner was cold? Do you? Do *YOU*?" He kicked her rear end with all his might. Elaina cried out in pain.

"Get up you lazy bitch! We've got some unfinished business."

"Noooo!" she cried.

"I passed out in the kitchen last night and didn't get my fill. C'mon woman. Into my bed."

Elaina trembled as she stood up, crossed her arms and started the slow march toward the bedroom. She closed her eyes for a second and remembered the beauty of her walk. At least if I die today, she thought, I had those moments of peace by the creek.

~ Chapter 9 ~

They wanted the truth.

Walt called Sgt. Wilcox at the Sheriff's Department and told him what Zahir had found out about Mitch's lies. With so little information to give him, Sgt. Wilcox suggested that Walt get something with Mitch's fingerprints to run through the database of convicted felons.

"Does this kid have any guns?"

Walt grimaced. "God, I hope not. I can ask Elaina, but I don't want to frighten her."

"Well, get the fingerprints and any other information that could provide us some clues."

"I recall one thing. He said he grew up in the North Country, along the St. Lawrence. A little town called Riverton."

"Hold on a second, Walt. Let me get the atlas." After a few minutes, Sgt. Wilcox picked up the phone. "Bad news, Walt. There's no such place."

When Walt got to the diner the Monday morning, he noticed something was weird about the way Elaina walked.

"Are you limping?"

"No, my rear is sore. That's all. I must have pulled a muscle when I slipped in the kitchen the other night."

"By the way, sorry I interrupted your dinner Saturday night. How come you didn't call me back yesterday?"

Elaina rubbed her sore elbow.

"Pop, I'm very sorry that Mitch was so rude to you when you called. He was nervous about making a good impression on his boss, Dick Baburka. And...we were busy yesterday. I forgot to call back. I'm sorry."

"Ah, that explains his anger then." Walt said looking at the wall. He tried to not show any judgment toward Mitch, so he could glean information for Sgt. Wilcox. It was very tough, though.

She stopped rolling the pie dough and looked at her father with sadness in her eyes that made him want to cry. Walt smiled gently at her.

"No need to apologize, daughter. So what are Mitch's work hours these days? That was pretty late for dinner time."

"Sometimes it's 9 to 5. Sometimes he leaves work and doesn't come home until 10. He says they have to be flexible for the clients. Most of them have day jobs."

"Is he home this morning?"

"No, he left real early. They're showing some big house on the South Side of Binghamton at seven this morning because the client has to catch a flight out of town. He was meeting Dick at a downtown diner to go over their plans."

Walt walked back toward the griddle and after a few minutes called back to her.

"Elaina, do you have a waffle iron at home? Looks like this one is on the fritz."

"Yes. Mitch likes waffles for Sunday breakfast. Want me to run home and get it?"

"No bother. You have pies to bake. Let me take your keys and I'll get it. Be right back."

"OK, they're in the pocket inside my purse."

As soon as Walt unlocked their apartment, he searched for something that might have Mitch's fingerprints. He saw the TV remote, but knew that would be missed immediately by his son-in-law. There were two coffee mugs in the sink. Which one was Mitch's? He'd miss that quickly, too. The rest of the kitchen was very tidy. Elaina's pride in a clean home was just like her mother's, he thought. Nothing in the living room was portable. No books. There was a set of weights in the corner, but they were too big. He needed to find something Mitch wouldn't miss. In the bathroom, he found his cologne. Nope. Too messy. Finally, in the bedroom on the dresser was a men's comb. Walt pulled out a plastic sandwich bag, inverted it and picked the comb up without his fingers touching it.

"Find it OK?" Elaina called out when he returned.

"Right where you said it would be. Thanks."

Angie had the day off, so it was just Mary Jo and Elaina waiting on tables. Once Elaina went in the dining room to take some orders, Walt called Sgt. Wilcox. He said he'd stop by later to pick up the comb.

Zahir was glad to see the sheriff's cruiser at the diner. That meant Walt had acted on the news he gave him, he thought. While he was looking out the window of the garage, a motorcycle pulled in followed by a car. It was Mitch and Dick Baburka.

"Elaina told me to bring the bike by so you could take a

look. The brakes have been acting funny. Could you check it out while we have a bite to eat across the street?"

Zahir had a car in the bay already, but didn't want to do anything that might trigger Mitch's wrath.

"Yes," he said with a forced smile. "Of course." He hated the way Mitch glared at him as if he was a terrorist, like so many others did these days. His college professor parents had been here since the 1960s. *When will we finally be considered Americans?*

Walt slipped the comb to Sgt. Wilcox just as Mitch and Dick crossed the road.

"Hang on Sergeant," Walt whispered. "The suspect is the tall fella just coming through the door." Walt wandered back to the kitchen.

"Mitch? What are you doing here?" Elaina said as she handed Sgt. Wilcox the blueberry pie he'd ordered. Mitch leaned over the counter to kiss her cheek. She backed away slightly and Sgt. Wilcox saw the fading bruises on her forehead and wrist.

"Well, the brakes were acting funny on my motorcycle," Mitch said, "and you're always telling me what a good mechanic Zahir is, so I thought I'd give him a try. Got any apple pie, yet? Dick and I could sure use a couple slices and some coffee."

"Have a seat, fellas," Walt said through the order window as he pointed at the stools next to Sgt. Wilcox at the counter. "Sgt. Wilcox, this here's my son-in-law Mitch Johnson."

"That's Petty Officer Third Class Mitch Johnson," he said

shaking the sheriff's deputy's hand. "And this is my boss Dick Baburka from Parlor City Realty." Mitch hunched his shoulders as he sat on the stool next to Sgt. Wilcox.

"Are you local, Mitch?"

"Nope. From the North Country."

"Walt said you've returned recently from the war. Thank you for your service."

Mitch sat back on the stool and puffed his chest.

"You know, I love this country, sergeant. It's been a privilege to serve her."

"What carrier were you on? My cousin's in the Persian Gulf right now."

Mitch looked around the diner then leaned in to whisper to him.

"Special Ops. Can't disclose where I was, what I was doing."

Sgt. Wilcox smiled and nodded. "I understand. Been involved in a few of them myself." He stood up, placed his money on the counter and called out to Walt.

"Well, gotta run. A speed trap beckons out there somewhere. Nice to see you again, Walt."

"Glad you could stop by, Sgt. Wilcox. It's been a long time. We appreciate your business and your service."

"You bet." Sgt. Wilcox tipped his hat toward Mitch and Dick. "Have a good day, gentlemen."

It didn't take Zahir long to find the leak. As he plugged it up and replaced the fluid, the thought crossed his mind that it would be so easy to sabotage Mitch's motorcycle. He could picture Mitch riding down the mountain and losing control, crashing and the motorcycle exploding. Then he thought what if some innocent person got in the way and was killed too? What if it was Elaina? He shook his head. He'd never had dark thoughts like this before. This motorcycle must be permeated by Mitch's evil aura.

Mitch came by to pick up his motorcycle and took out his wallet to pay Zahir.

"You owe nothing. Elaina and Walt are like family to me."

Mitch frowned.

"She ain't your family, bud. I appreciate the gesture just the same."

Zahir noticed a heavy wrench on the wall just behind Mitch. If he lunged forward and grabbed it, he could bash in Mitch's skull. He shook his head. I *am* picking up evil vibes from this jerk, he thought.

Mitch glowered as he replayed Zahir's words, "like family," in his mind. Those words from Zahir simmered over Mitch's hot plate of anger all day. He'd have to fix that punk A-rab for flirting with his wife. There were all sorts of witnesses at the diner who'd confirm he was having his brakes fixed at Zahir's while eating lunch at the diner. It would be so easy to frame him. After dark, he rode the motorcycle up by the airport and turned up an abandoned road he remembered near an empty farmhouse. He drained the brake fluid from the reservoir, rode the bike back slowly to the road and looked around where he could create an accident scene. Straight ahead was a slight hill with a field on the right. An old beech tree grew right by the shoulder. Mitch started up the motorcycle, gathered enough speed as he pointed it toward the tree then jumped off into the field just before it smashed into the tree.

Perfect. The motorcycle was a mess. He'd scuffed up his clothes enough to look like it'd really happened and a fallen branch cut his lip when he landed on it. He spit into his hands, bent down and made some mud with dirt on the road's shoulder. Then he hit the heels of his hands across his face and into his hair to enhance his look of distress.

* * *

"I've had an accident. Just around the bend. Brakes failed," Mitch said to the cashier at the convenience store up the road. She ran to get a wet washcloth for his face, sat him down and called 911.

"The thing is, my brakes were just worked on today by that Arab fella across from the diner near the airport," Mitch told the sheriff's deputy. "I'm a war vet, so I guess I'm a bit paranoid, but you don't suppose he tampered with them?"

* * *

When Elaina arrived to pick up Mitch, he told her he was going to need her car for work. She could get a ride with Walt until the motorcycle was repaired.

"We're never taking our vehicles to Zahir again. I swear he tampered with my brakes. Tell that to your father, too."

"Zahir would never do anything like that. He's a good person," she pouted.

"That's just the way them A-rabs are. I saw it firsthand over there in the war. They're all nice and calling you a hero one second, next thing you know they're setting off IEDs next to your convoy and your buddy is dead. No sense of loyalty."

"Why would someone in the Navy be in a convoy?"

"I told you, I can't disclose what I did over there."

Still didn't make any sense to her. Ugh, she thought. If she went to work when Pop did that would mean she'd be getting home later and Mitch would be angrier.

"Can't Dick give you a ride to work?"

"I can't believe this. Here I am injured and you're whining that I have to use your car. Besides, you don't need your car once you're at work. I'm constantly on the road. Even a dummy could figure out that." They walked in the apartment and Mitch went right over to the lounge chair.

"Grab me a beer, sugarplum."

God, Elaina hated that word! She hated it even more than her husband's touch. Who was this stranger she'd been living with? Oh how she wished they'd never met.

* * *

Butch Polakovich was at the counter the next morning reading the racetrack paper as he sipped coffee. He happened to look up at the mirror behind the counter and saw a reflection of the sheriff's car across the road.

"What's the sheriff doing over there? Checking immigration papers?"

"I've told you a million times, Butch," Walt pointed at him with the spatula. "Those people are Americans, just like you and me. Zahir's a fine mechanic, too."

"Oh yeah? Well I heard he tried to kill some guy by

draining all the fluid out of his motorcycle brakes."

"Where did you hear that nonsense? That's a lie."

"People are talking, that's all. Sorry to burst your bubble. You know, you'd be wise to not trust everyone you meet, Walt. Keep an eye on your own brakes, too."

Elaina was looking out the window and saw the sheriff's deputy speaking with Zahir. Walt came over and put his arm around her.

"Oh, Pop. You don't think Zahir would do anything like that to Mitch. Do you?"

"Not for a second. Of course he wouldn't. Probably the plug fell out or maybe Mitch drove over something and it somehow sprang a leak."

"Is that young man being questioned about the missing woman?" a customer in a nearby booth asked them.

"What missing woman?" Walt asked.

"I think her name is Kirsten Anderson. She's a barmaid at the Glenmere. Lives around here somewhere. No one's seen her since Saturday night."

Elaina was half paying attention. She was so upset about Zahir. In fact, she noticed at that moment that she was far more upset about Zahir than she was about her husband's wreck.

"What did you say about the Glenmere?"

The woman pointed at a story in the newspaper. There was a photo of the woman—very pretty. She'd been seen talking with two men in the parking lot after the bar closed. No one had seen her since.

A sudden wave of queasiness overcame Elaina. What if Mitch and Dick went back to the Glenmere on Saturday night after she fell asleep? Could they be responsible for her disappearance? She thought about telling her father about it, but hesitated. Elaina hated the thought of stirring up more trouble.

After lunch, a woman dressed in a lime green shirtwaist dress with pearls, gloves, a wide-brimmed floral hat and sunglasses sat down in a booth with her back to the door. She was definitely not the type of customer one was used to seeing in the diner. The women in the booth next to her figured she was one of those hoity-toitys who live on Riverside Drive in Binghamton.

"May I have some tea, Earl Grey if you have it," the woman said as she took off her gloves and accepted the menu Elaina handed her. Elaina went off to look through that special box of tea they kept under the counter—they didn't get much call for Earl Grey—when she heard someone sit down nearby.

"Hey, sugarplum." The words sent a chill through her. She turned around and saw Mitch and Dick park themselves at the counter.

"So has anyone stopped by to visit your dear friend Zahir today? Say a sheriff's deputy?"

"I haven't noticed. Mary Jo's off on vacation and it's very busy here today." She brushed past them and brought tea to the woman in green.

Mitch looked at his reflection and noticed the wind had mussed his hair. "Could I borrow your comb a second, boss. I must have misplaced mine at home."

Dick handed his comb to Mitch as he watched the mysterious woman speaking with Elaina.

"Who's the classy broad in the booth?" he asked.

Mitch turned around to look. "Dunno. Never seen her in here before." He elbowed his boss. "You oughta go over and work some of that Baburka magic on her."

"Think I should? What if she's got a face like a dog, though? Don't ya hate that? You see some chick walking down the street with her hips swayin' oh so sweet, and then she turns around and it's bow-wow-wow!"

The two men looked at each other, threw their heads back and howled like wolves. Diners stopped eating, mid fork, turned around and stared at them. The mysterious woman didn't budge and just sipped her tea, pinky out.

"Are you ready to order, ma'am?" Elaina asked. She wondered why the woman kept her sunglasses on.

"I should order something light because I'm watching my figure, but I've heard the pie here is decadent and delicious. What do you recommend?"

"Customers seem to prefer the apple, but today I also have a peanut butter fluff, banana cream and key lime."

"Ooh, how will I ever make up my mind with such temptation?" she laughed. Elaina thought her laugh sounded a bit familiar but she was sure she'd never met her before. C'mon lady, she thought, I've got so many customers in here.

"Oh, I know I shouldn't but let's go with the peanut butter fluff. Calories be damned." Elaina grinned as she went out back to the kitchen and pointed out the woman to her father.

"Who is she, Pop? Some sort of food critic from the paper or TV?"

"I don't know. She looks kinda familiar."

Mitch elbowed his boss again. "Go ahead. Make your move. Get the flowers from that vase and take her a bouquet. Chicks always dig flowers."

Dick jumped off the stool, grabbed the handful of wildflowers Elaina had picked from the side of the road, adjusted the comb-over atop his head and walked over to the woman in green like a cowboy strutting into a saloon.

"Flowers for milady," he said bowing toward her as he extended the impromptu bouquet.

"Oh," the woman smiled, "but they're dripping wet...."

Dick leaned in close to her.

"That's just how I could leave you tonight, baby, if you let me take you for a ride."

You could hear the slap echo throughout the diner. Customers laughed out loud at Dick as he slunk back to the counter stool. Elaina rushed over to the mystery woman.

"Ma'am, I'm so sorry if that man insulted you. Trust me; he's not a regular customer here. I hope you won't blame us."

The woman turned and looked at Dick and Mitch.

"I don't know *why* he would assume that I was *that* kind of woman."

"Of course you're not. I have no idea why he was so rude. That type of thing doesn't happen here. It's probably the first time he's seen a real lady."

The woman patted Elaina's hand.

"Now that's not true. After all, he's seen you in here."

She brought a big smile to Elaina's face.

"Thank you, ma'am. That was very kind of you to say."

Elaina wrote out the check for Dick and Mitch and slammed it on the counter.

"Hey, what happened to the family discount?" Mitch said angrily.

"Consider this a fine for your boss's disgusting behavior and disturbing the peace in our diner," she snarled back with uncustomary sarcasm. Inside Elaina was jumping up and down—she finally found the courage to speak her mind to Mitch about that jerk.

"Man, I go across the street and get the motorcycle repaired and Zahir says no charge for family. But my own wife charges us for two lousy pieces of pie and coffee?"

Elaina smirked. "He said that?"

Dick sniggered. "Yeah, no charge for family 'cause I'll just kill you for free."

This time her inner voice told her don't say another word, just walk away. She heeded it, wisely, and went back into the kitchen.

"Pop, did you hear what Mitch just said?" she whispered. "Zahir didn't charge Mitch for the brake work on the motorcycle. Said there was no charge for family."

Walt raised an eyebrow and smiled.

"Why would he say that to my husband if he was planning to kill him?"

"Of course Zahir's innocent. Never doubted it. I'll be sure to tell that to Sgt. Wilcox. And don't worry, Elaina. I don't think any charges are going to be filed."

She was relieved to see the two men were gone by the time she came back out into the dining room. The mystery woman had finished her pie and Elaina brought over her check.

"That was a slice of heaven, child. You couldn't find pie that good in the best restaurants in Manhattan."

"You think so? Really?" *Ohmigod, maybe she is a restaurant critic,* Elaina thought. "I'm so glad you enjoyed it. Anything else I can get you?"

"Don't they let you take a break around here?"

Elaina looked at the clock. "Well, actually, my break should have started ten minutes ago."

"Sit down with me then, a second. Can I buy you a cup of coffee?"

Elaina put up her hand.

"No thanks, I'm fine. If you don't mind I will sit down, though." She plopped into the booth across from the nice woman.

"You know, I have to say that I'm very disappointed about one thing."

Oh no, Elaina thought. Here it comes. She *is* a food critic. Or worse, maybe she's a food inspector with the state. She sat up straight.

"What? Didn't you like the crust?"

"You don't seem to recognize me."

Elaina blushed.

"To be honest, ma'am, I was just saying to Pop that you looked familiar. Have I seen you on TV or in the paper?"

"Yes, I'm in the arts," then the woman's voice dropped to a lower register, "I own the gallery down the road." She removed her sunglasses and Elaina recognized Rhey. She started laughing hysterically which made the diners turn around and stare at them.

"Oh...my...God, Rhey! You are *insane!*"

"Gotcha, Elly." A huge grin burst across Rhey's face. Elaina shook her head.

"Man you were good. So mysterious. Where did you get the fancy hat and dress? Look at that eye makeup, you look like a starlet."

Rhey struck a dramatic pose.

"Oh, these old things? Remnants of my dinner theater days. Aren't they wonderful?"

"That was Mitch at the counter right now. You'd be dead if he found out it was you."

"*No!* Was he the brute who just attempted to hit on me?"

Elaina rolled her eyes. "No. That'd be Mitch's boss. Two peas in a pod, I'd say."

Rhey took Elaina's hands and looked at her face. He noticed the fading black and blues.

"What happened to your forehead? Are those bruises?"

Elaina pulled her hair forward to cover it up.

"And your wrist, too?" Rhey said with alarm.

She looked away out the window.

"There's a matching one on my rear. From Mitch's shoe."

Rhey reached out with his hands and cupped her face.

"Oh, Elly. How long has this been going on? I've wondered why you never called me."

Elaina looked down at the table top and started playing with the salt and pepper shakers.

"It just started last week. The physical stuff, that is. He screams at me pretty much every day."

Rhey gasped. He touched her hand.

"Why don't you leave him, El? Come back into the light with the rest of us. You shouldn't be wasting your life trapped in domestic hell."

"You know, I've thought about it. Many times. I think I haven't acted on it because I'm more afraid of what he'd do to Pop, you and even Zahir while he's out looking for me."

"This is crazy. It's no way to live. You have to save yourself and leave him. Heaven knows what he's capable of doing."

"I know...." Her lips trembled as tears welled in her eyes.

"By the way, what were the cops doing over at Zahir's?"

"Mitch had an accident on his motorcycle the other night. Brakes failed. Earlier in the day he'd had Zahir look at them because he thought they were leaking fluid. Mitch says Zahir tried to kill him. He told the sheriff that Zahir didn't seem to like him because he was a patriot and had probably killed some of his distant cousins."

"Ugh, Mitch, give that patriot act a rest, will ya? There's no way sweet Zahir would do anything like that." Rhey noticed how much his dear friend Elaina had aged in the past months. "I wouldn't blame him if he thought about it, though."

She laughed.

"So how are the plans for Simon's exhibit going?"

"Slowly. He told me I could connect the stories they tell, but so far I can't decide what connects them. I think I'm just few more pitchers of daiquiris away from sorting it all out."

* * *

When the sheriff's deputy left Zahir's garage, he headed down Airport Road toward the scene of the accident. As he passed an abandoned road and saw the old farmhouse in the distance, he thought about that barmaid reported missing. He recalled that she lived not too far from here. Instinct made the deputy turn onto the muddy road where he noticed fresh single tire tracks, the width of a motorcycle's. He followed them halfway to the house where they ended abruptly. He got out of the cruiser to look around and noticed there was some amber-colored fluid spilled on the ground. The deputy pulled out a piece of paper, curved it and scraped some of the fluid up.

"My, my, my...could this be brake fluid?"

He called into headquarters on the cruiser's radio.

"Draper here. Any word on that missing barmaid?"

"She's OK. Turned up this afternoon. Guess she'd had some sort of spat with her boyfriend and was hiding at her friend's house."

"Glad to hear that. Say, I think there's something interesting up here connected to that motorcycle crash by the airport. I just found what looks like brake fluid dumped about a quarter mile away from the accident site."

"Did you interview the mechanic?"

"Yes. I don't think he tampered with the brakes. I do wonder if the rider dumped the fluid then tried to stage an accident for some reason. The fluid is on an abandoned dirt road, right near the airport. There's an old farmhouse nearby."

"Stop by the garage and get a sample of the brake fluid he used and get a sample of what you found. We'll run them through the lab and see what comes up."

~ Chapter 10 ~

It was a call she never expected.

Maria was brushing down her quarter horse mare when she heard the phone ringing in the house. She ran inside to pick it up.

"Hello?" she said breathlessly.

There was silence on the other end for a couple seconds.

"Mom, is that you?"

Maria put her hand over her pounding heart.

"Who is this?"

"It's your daughter, Dee Dee."

Maria gasped and put her hand over her mouth.

"Mom? You there?"

"How did you get this number?"

The words stung Dee Dee. They hadn't spoken in more than a decade and these were the first words her mother said to her? Had she made an awful mistake by calling Maria?

"Pop said you were living in Missoula," she said hesitatingly. "So I googled your name with Missoula and found an article about you winning a prize at that horse show. Remember when you used to take me and Elaina to the stables by the diner on Sunday afternoons?"

Maria took the phone into the living room and sat down on the couch.

"Listen, honey, I didn't mean to be so curt just now. I'm so sorry for all...I just had to do what I did back then because.... Walt's such a good, decent man and I'm sure he's been a great father to you, but...well, I just felt like that diner was suffocating me. I couldn't stand the routine. Bake the same pies every day. Wipe down the same booths. Make endless small talk with the same boring customers. How I *hated* it. It probably sounds silly and like it's not enough of an excuse for what I did to you. I hope you and your sister can forgive me."

Dee Dee didn't know what to say. Part of her was relieved. Her mom had left because of the diner's drudgery, *not* anything she'd done as a dumb little kid. For years she carried the guilt that her brattiness toward Elaina drove Maria away. Dumb little kid thoughts, she realized.

Dee Dee's silence made Maria sigh.

"Oh dear, I didn't mean to blurt all that out. Let me start again, Dee Dee. How are you and your sister doing? You've got a birthday coming up soon, right? Twenty-four?"

"Yeah." Dee Dee was surprised she even remembered that. Maria never sent them birthday cards or Christmas presents after she left. Pop got a call from her every once in a while, to make sure they were still alive, she guessed. After their divorce, Maria never left a phone number or an address where they could contact her though.

"Why are you calling? Is Walt all right? And Elaina?"

"We're OK, Mom. I have some news and just thought you might want to know, that's all."

"What?"

"I got married. To a wonderful guy. His name is Joachim and he's from Germany. He plays the cello like I do and we live in Boston now."

Maria's heart leapt. She smiled and thought yes, those music lessons had done their job. Maybe she wasn't such a horrible mother after all.

"You sound very happy, Dee Dee. I bet he's cute, too."

Dee Dee giggled. *"Very.* Mom, he's the kindest, gentlest man. He's a lot like Pop."

Maria knew it wasn't Dee Dee's intention, but those words stung. Yes, she'd felt guilty for years leaving a man who'd been as good to her as Walt had been. But he just couldn't see that there was more to life than that damn diner. The man she left him for—Mort—was very kind also. She could see the two of them becoming fast friends if they could get past the awkwardness of it all. They were very different in one way, though. Mort wasn't a stay-put sort of man. He drove eighteen-wheelers across the country and thrived on the new experiences his travels brought to his life. Sometimes Maria would join him on a run, and she saw why he enjoyed it so much. More often than not she'd stay put on their ranch in Missoula. Give her wide open prairies, fluffy clouds in a big turquoise sky and she was happy.

"I have more news, Mom. Elaina's married too."

Maria was shocked. She felt an ache in her heart. Both daughters married and she'd never met their husbands. What a terrible mother she'd been.

"She eloped to Niagara Falls with this sailor just back from the war. They came right back home and she's been working with Pop at the diner ever since. All the customers love her pies."

Maria cringed. Her oldest was following the path she first took. She could almost feel Elaina's sense of entrapment way out here in Montana.

"What's he like?"

"Want me to be honest?"

"Of course."

"He's a total jerk. Bosses her around. Won't let her talk on the phone to me if it's around his dinner time. I think he just married her so he could have a steady supply of her pies."

"Yes, men like pie," Maria said, words drifting off as she stared toward the snowcapped Bitterroot Mountains in the distance. Oh her poor Elaina. What possessed her to teach her oldest daughter the family pie recipe? It was more of a curse than a family keepsake.

"How are you, Mom? How's your hus...I mean boy...um, partner?"

"Mort is just fine. Thanks for asking, Dee Dee. You'll have to come out here with Joachim and meet him. I think you'd like him. He's a kind man and we have a wonderful life together here on the ranch. You'd fall in love with this place. The scenery is so beautiful it doesn't seem real. I bet you'd be inspired to write some music here."

"Great idea. Maybe Joachim and I could take an epic road trip out there sometime. That'd be so *awesome*."

Maria laughed at her daughter's enthusiasm.

"Anyway, the reason why I'm calling is that Pop's having a party to celebrate our marriages. It's going to be held the second Sunday in September at the diner. I know this is kinda crazy and out of the blue, but I was wondering if you two would like to join us."

She said "you two." That made Maria smile. Maybe they hadn't prejudged Mort.

"It doesn't sound like anyone wants to celebrate Elaina's marriage though."

"Well, you know Pop. He's always diplomatic. He doesn't want to hurt her feelings or make her feel left out."

Maria nodded. Walt was always able to see past people's faults—including hers—and was slow to judge people.

"Do you think you and Mort would be able to come? It'd be your wedding gift to us. Elaina really *needs* you, Mom."

Dee Dee's plea jarred Maria. She hadn't heard that word directed at her in years. Why did Dee Dee think her opinions would matter to Elaina? Immediately, she felt trapped by a burden she'd buried under new memories. The thought of stepping back into the place that symbolized the imprisonment she once felt held no attraction for Maria. However, she heard a tone in Dee Dee's voice that tugged at her heart as if there was something she wasn't telling her that might be of concern. Dee Dee must be desperate if she's calling me, Maria thought.

"I'll talk it over with Mort and see what he says."

"Really? Oh Mom, that would be fantastic! I haven't told anyone I'm doing this, so if you come it would be a huge surprise. Please come. *Please.*"

"No one knows about this? Oh, Dee Dee. I'm not sure that your father would agree about it being fantastic. You should ask him if it's OK. I don't want to hurt him anymore than I have already." Maria was trapped. She didn't want to disappoint her daughter yet again.

"Oh, Dad's doing fine," Dee Dee lied. "He's very laid back. I bet he'd be cool about it."

Maria didn't believe her.

"We'll see what we can do. It was lovely talking with you, Dee Dee. I'm proud of you for your success. You take care now."

"You too, Mom. I love you."

Dee Dee hung up before Maria could respond. I love you too, she thought as she carried the phone back into the kitchen and walked out onto the porch. A steady breeze was flowing down the mountains across the valley, carrying the scent of sagebrush. It was quiet except for the song of a lone bobolink atop the corral fence.

"What just happened?" Maria said to the bird. For years she'd been living out here free as a mustang, her days spent lazily with the horses or enjoying her new hobby, painting. Then in an instant one phone call reached out like a lasso from the East and drew taut around her heart. That rope of a phone line transmitted instantly bad memories, stress, heartache and restlessness she'd thought she'd left behind in the parking lot of The Terminal Diner. How could she go back? What would she say to Walt when she'd see him for the first time since she left? Sorry for dumping you and the girls, but the diner was destroying me? Could he possibly understand that it was nothing personal?

* * *

Walt picked up the phone at the diner.

"Hi, Sgt. Wilcox. What can I do for you?"

"Just wanted to let you know that we were able to get some fingerprints off that comb."

"Great. Any luck identifying him?"

"So far they haven't matched any prints in the local database. We're going to run them in the state one, so hopefully they'll trigger a match there."

"Maybe he's from out of state."

"There's something else, Walt. One of our deputies came across some dumped brake fluid. It was on a road about a quarter mile away from Mitch's wreck."

"What are you saying? Did he fake his accident?"

"That's one scenario we're investigating."

"Holy crap! Why would he do that?"

"Does he hate that mechanic? Would he want to frame him for some reason?"

"Zahir is a good friend of mine. And Elaina's. There's nothing between them, though."

"OK. Thanks again for the comb, Walt. Don't worry. We'll find out all we can about this guy."

"Thanks. You guys do great work. By the way, what did you think of Elaina's bruises?"

The sergeant paused. "They're definitely not from a fall, Walt. I've seen this too many times. Listen; let me give you the

- 173 -

phone number for the Women's Safe Haven. Elaina might need it someday soon."

"Thanks, Sergeant," Walt said, rubbing his brow. "I'll make sure she gets it."

* * *

Someone knocked on the front door of Elaina's apartment that night. It was past 9:30 and she wondered why anyone would be at her door.

"May I help you?" Elaina said.

"Deputy Draper, ma'am, from the Sheriff's Department. Sgt. Wilcox asked me to stop by and ask your husband some more questions about his accident."

"He's not home yet from work. I'm not sure when he will show up."

"Mind if I come in and ask you a few questions?"

"Of course not. Come in."

She wondered why the deputy kept asking so many questions about her relationship with Zahir. Did he think somehow that she'd asked Zahir to tamper with the brakes? Did he suspect that they were romantically involved and he was looking for a reason why Zahir might do it? Uh-oh, had she somehow been giving Zahir the idea that she was interested in him?

She thought about how their friendship had started, that day he towed her car out of the ditch. Sure they were friends, but not in the way she was friends with Rhey. If Rhey wasn't gay, Mitch would definitely have something to worry about.

"Do you have any idea where your husband is? Does he

come home late often?"

"I never know when he's going to show up anymore. He says it's the nature of the business of selling homes. But I've been wondering who would be looking at a house so late at night."

The deputy gave her a look that she thought meant she was missing something obvious.

"You know, he often goes to that bar on Main Street in Binghamton, the Glenmere, with his boss Dick Baburka. They stop by after work for a few beers, he says."

He smirked. "All right. Sorry to bother you. Please have your husband call me at this number when he gets in," he said handing her a business card. "I'm on the night shift tonight, so don't worry that it might be too late to call. Thanks for your time, ma'am."

* * *

Deputy Draper decided to take a detour past the Glenmere on his way back to headquarters. Sure enough, he saw a car matching Elaina's license plate and description in the parking lot. He parked his cruiser on a shady side street where he had a clear view of the parking lot. He didn't have to wait too long. Mitch came out with his arm draped around a young woman wearing an apron. They staggered down the steps and walked around to the side of the bar. Mitch pressed the woman against the building and kissed her forcefully. The woman didn't appear to be resisting and responded willingly enough. He pulled out some binoculars in his glove compartment so he could get a better look at her face and was disturbed by what he saw. She was the same barmaid, Kirsten Anderson, who'd been reported missing recently.

"What a jerk," Deputy Draper said. He waited until they went back into the bar then drove to headquarters where he planned to read the missing person file on Kirsten.

* * *

Elaina was tired of waiting up for Mitch. She left the meat loaf in a pan on the stove and went to bed. He could help himself and reheat it when he came in. A few hours later, she was roused from her sleep by the sound of pots banging in the kitchen. No, she thought, I'm not going in there. I'm tired of being pushed around by him.

"Where the hell's my hot meal? Dammit! I hate cold meat loaf!" Mitch screamed. "Lazy wife can't wait up for her husband and serve him a decent meal. Damn BITCH!" He slammed a cupboard door so hard she could feel the concussion from it shake the bedroom wall.

Something glass broke. Elaina's heart was pounding. Should she get up and lock the bedroom door? Would she have time to slide the dresser in front of it to ensure he couldn't get in? Wouldn't the noise attract him and maybe he'd attack her with a broken glass before she could secure the room?

Mitch slammed the refrigerator door and she heard him pop open a can of beer. It was silent for a few minutes except for her beating heart that sounded so loud to her she wondered if he could hear it, too. She lay on her bed, paralyzed with terror, fearing even her shallow breathing might draw him near to harm her.

He belched and threw the beer can on the floor. Then she heard him dialing someone on his cell phone.

"Hey baby, it's me. Whatchya doin'? I'm hungry. Wanna go get breakfast somewhere? OK, then. I'll be there soon."

She could hear Mitch's shoes crunching the broken glass as he walked over to the sink and turned on the water. Next she heard the jingle of car keys. His foot caught the beer can and spun it down the hall toward the bedroom. The front door opened and slammed shut. A car engine started. Silence.

She waited a few minutes to be sure that it was her car that had pulled away. Her heart was still pounding as she slid gently off the bed, stuck her feet into slippers and tiptoed toward the kitchen. She picked up the beer can and looked around the corner. The floor was a mess. A hunk of meat loaf with a bite taken out of it lay on the floor where he had thrown it down in disgust. Glass shards were mashed with potatoes.

Elaina peeked out the front door window and saw that her car was gone. Ohmigod, she thought as she sank to the floor shaking. She curled up in a fetal position and sat on the floor rocking back and forth. I can't live like this, she thought. I can't live like this. Rhey is right; I have to get back into the light. Can't live like this. Can't live. Can't. She sat there rocking for a few minutes then remembered Mitch's conversation. Who is she? Who is "baby"? Where is she? Who?

Fear morphed into anger. Part of her wanted to leave the mess where it was. That's what he deserves for going off with some *chick*. Part of her feared the consequences of what would happen to her if he returned, sober, and found the mess still there. She rocked some more. *I want out of this. I can't do this anymore. I want out. Out!*

She stood up, grabbed a mop and then a broom, and cleaned the floor. A weird thing happened. Her thoughts turned to her mother and what she must have been thinking the day she left Pop. How did she work up the nerve to abandon them all? Elaina knew her father had never treated her mother like Mitch did her. Yet, she was able to just walk away. Was it something she'd been planning for a while or was it an impulsive decision? Would she be able to do the same thing her mother did? She could call a cab and take the first Greyhound out of Binghamton. She'd hate to abandon her father, leaving him in a tough position like that. Her elopement was hard enough on him. Elaina knew she'd miss Rhey and Zahir, too. Heck, she'd even miss the continuing saga that was Mary Jo's life. That made her laugh.

Elaina tried to remember what it was like that day her mother left. When the afternoon school bus dropped her and Dee Dee off at the diner, Maria wasn't waiting by the cash register to greet them as usual. Then they saw Pop sitting in the booth staring at a note in his hand and Angie rubbing his back. He grabbed them both up into his arms and hugged them tightly.

"Girls...your mother has gone. Left us. I'm so sorry. I don't know how she could do this to us."

Later he told them the specifics. She had waited on Mort and they had some sort of instant chemistry. Walt happened to glance out the order window and saw her giggling as she whispered something in Mort's ear. Then she touched his arm and her hand lingered there forever it seemed to Walt. He was distracted by a big order that Angie gave him and when he looked back, Mort was gone. He found Maria's note taped to the refrigerator a few minutes after that. She must have slipped out the back door and met him in the parking lot.

For years Elaina wondered why her mother did it. Like Dee Dee, she wondered if her mother was sick and tired of their bickering and just had to get away. Every once in a while she wondered what her mother was doing at the moment, was she having some wonderful adventure? Elaina even daydreamed that she was a secret agent and had to flee town for reasons that couldn't be told. After her marriage to Mitch, she gained a new perspective. Her hurt from abandonment morphed into admiration. *Mom had the courage I wish I had.*

Elaina looked at the clock. Her workday started in an hour. Mitch still wasn't back and she sure wasn't anxious to wait for his return. She called a taxi. The sooner she got out of this hellhole, the better.

After she showered, she got dressed and thought, you know what, I'm going to wear that scarf Rhey gave me. Just to spite the sleazy bastard. She opened the drawer where she kept her few accessories, but it wasn't there. That's odd, she thought. Where else would I have put it? She shuffled through the rest of her dresser drawers. It wasn't there. Wait, didn't she put it in the kitchen drawer? She walked out to the kitchen and rifled through the catch-all drawer but it wasn't there.

Elaina tried to visualize the last place she'd seen it.

Definitely in her bedroom, but where? She checked the closet, looking inside everything hanging up in case she'd draped it on a hanger she used for something else. Not there. Come to think of it, maybe she hadn't seen it since the day Rhey gave it to her. Could Mitch have taken it?

She crossed the room to his dresser. It was the first time she'd opened it, he'd been so territorial about it. Her scarf wasn't in the top drawer. Nor the second. In the way back of the bottom drawer she saw bright blue fabric peeking out from under his khaki trousers. She opened the drawer all the way and lifted up the pants. It was her scarf, all right. And it was wrapped around a revolver.

Elaina was afraid to touch the scarf. Was the drawer booby-trapped so if she tried to pull the scarf out, the gun would go off? She stepped back and started biting her finger nail. "I love that scarf, I need that scarf, you bastard! I've gotta get the hell out of here!"

She pushed the drawer back in slowly, grabbed a small suitcase and packed it with enough clothes to last a week. As she waited for the taxi to pick her up, she looked around the apartment to see if there was anything there that she couldn't live without if she never came back. Yia Yia's cookbook, she thought. The photo of her, Dee Dee and Pop in front of the diner, had to come, too. In her accessory drawer, she pulled out the scarf she was wearing the day she met Zahir and a paper parasol from the first daiquiri Rhey made her. The taxi driver beeped. She zipped up the suitcase, dashed through the apartment and opened the front door. Elaina paused, slipped her wedding ring off and threw it on the carpet where Mitch kicked her.

* * *

Zahir saw the taxi pull up across the road. That's odd at this hour. When he saw Elaina step out with a suitcase, he smiled broadly. It could mean only one thing.

Elaina hid the suitcase in a back closet seldom used at the diner. She put on her apron and looked around the kitchen to determine what she'd bake that day. If this was her last day at the diner, these were going to be her finest pies. How many times had she stood over that working surface, blending flour, shortening, salt and ice water? How many pies crusts had she rolled out here, lifted carefully into baking tins and filled with fresh fruit or custard fillings?

Once she stopped being sentimental about the moment, she considered her plan of action. She could be like her mother and hitch a ride with the first rig that pulled into the parking lot. She could book a seat on the first flight out of the airport. Pop, Dee Dee, Rhey and Zahir couldn't be told about her plans. Nor could Angie or Mary Jo. Any of them could face the wrath of Mitch if they knew where she was heading.

Then second guessing haunted her. Maybe it was a dumb decision to toss her wedding ring on the apartment floor. Mitch might find it and come looking for her right away at the diner. What would she do if he showed up?

Walt walked in the diner, touched his fingers on the lucky pound note and called out to her.

"Hi Pop," she answered, pretending it was just another

morning at the diner. He looked grim, and she feared he'd already been paid a visit by Mitch.

"Here. You might need this, Sgt. Wilcox said. It's the number of the Women's Safe Haven." Elaina took the slip of paper from her father. "Promise me, if you feel the slightest bit afraid, you'll go right there. OK?" He waited for her response. She knew at that moment that her father never believed the lies she told him about her bruises. He knew things had gotten out of control as well as she did. Elaina hugged her father. It was nice to know she had another escape possibility that would keep her in town.

"He still has your car?"

She nodded.

"I stopped by this morning to pick you up and you were gone. I waited outside the apartment for a few minutes then went to the door and rang the bell. I got pretty nervous when no one answered. I hoped you'd taken a taxi here."

"Sorry to frighten you, Pop. I should have called."

"Mitch is out early today. What's up with him?"

She considered confiding to him what had occurred but hesitated. It might be too risky still. Elaina just shrugged. It wasn't that easy to keep silent that day, though. A car backfired out on the road as it passed the diner and she ducked. Every time she heard a deep voice in the dining room she thought about the escape options available to her. Elaina was glad that her suitcase was close in case she needed it for that purpose.

* * *

Later that morning, a young man walked into the diner

carrying a bouquet of flowers.

"Excuse me, miss," he said to Angie. "Is the woman who makes the pies here today?"

Angie looked at the young man holding a stunning summer bouquet of fragrant daylilies and deep blue hydrangeas. What's that Mitch up to now, she wondered?

"I'd like to speak with her if she's in."

"Hold on a sec, hon." Angie went into the kitchen.

"Elaina, there's a kid out here with flowers to see you."

She dropped the rolling pin on the floor and looked like she'd just seen a ghost, Angie thought.

"Are they from Mitch? Is he out there?"

"I'm not sure. The kid wasn't driving a florist van. Do you have any other secret admirers?"

"No. What's this guy want?"

"He said he just wants to speak to you. That's all. Everything OK, hon? You look terrified."

"Come out there with me. OK?"

The young man was sitting at the counter with one hand on a beautiful crystal vase that held the bouquet. Elaina looked out the window to see if Mitch was lurking, but her car wasn't in the parking lot.

"Yes?" she said to him. "You wanted to see me?"

He squinted at her name tag and smiled.

"Elaina's your name. *That* was it. I was close. I remembered it as Amy. These are for you." He handed her the bouquet and the scent of the daylilies caught her off guard. It was an intoxicating scent. Angie leaned in for a sniff.

"Thank you," Elaina said as she took the vase from him slowly, still looking around for Mitch.

"You don't remember me, do you?"

Elaina looked at the young man blankly then back at Angie and shook her head.

"I can understand. It's been a few years. I should have come back here sooner but I have these issues with being near airports and low flying planes."

"Issues?"

"It was you who served me a lucky piece of apple pie, the best I'd ever tasted, the day before 9/11. I was heading off to an interview."

"Ohmigod! It's *you!*" Elaina set the vase on the counter and hugged the young man who'd come into the diner the day before the terrorist attacks. "You're alive? *You're alive!* Thank you, God! We never knew what happened to you because I didn't know your name, of course. I scoured the newspapers every day, hoping there'd be a photo of you. My friend Rhey had this vigil at the gallery and we mentioned you and everyone prayed for you. We thought you were dead. But you're not. You're here. I can't believe it. I'm so happy! Wow, wait until Rhey hears this."

"Rhey, he's the artist, right? The guy in the pink shirt? I remember he was a good painter."

"You remember him? We're like best friends now and we just met for the first time that day."

"Yeah, I remember that day in minute detail. And there was this sailor there, too. He was insulting Rhey. Remember?

You and I stood up for him."

Elaina had a flashback to that moment. She'd forgotten about the obnoxious sailor. Then she recalled she specifically read his name tag to remember what a jerk he was. His name was Johnson. *Johnson?* Ohmigod, it must have been Mitch. She put her hands over her mouth. How could she have forgotten him? He was so rude and insulting about Rhey. Of course the horrific events of the next day made her mind focus on little else. She felt like she'd been hit by a strong gust of wind and sat down on a stool at the counter.

Just then a plane landing at the airport flew in low. The young man cowered and held on to the edge of the counter, wincing.

"It's OK. That plane flies over every weekday at this time."

"I've been in therapy for quite a while. This was a big test for me, to see if I could come up here to see you and let you know I'm OK, and to thank you for the good luck you gave me."

"So tell us. What happened that day? Wait, let's sit in a booth. Can we get you something? Coffee? Pie?"

"I'm supposed to avoid caffeine. Not good for my nerves. A glass of milk would be fine. I would love another slice of that delicious apple pie if you have some." Elaina nodded to Angie and she went to get him milk and some pie as they sat down.

"First things first," Elaina said. "I'm Elaina Brady. What's your name?" Wow. She realized what she'd just said without missing a beat, that it had been effortless to divorce her name from Mitch's in her mind. That made her smile.

"Josh Connelly. Nice to meet you formally, Elaina Brady."

As they shook hands, Elaina noticed he was wearing a blue shirt. The dream...was this the moment it was all about?

Angie came back with the milk and pie then sat down in the booth, too. There were only a couple customers at the moment and they had just gotten their food a little while ago.

"Well, my first interview in Manhattan went very well that afternoon and they arranged for me to meet with the vice president of the firm the next morning at nine. His office was on the 60th floor of the North Tower of the World Trade Center. I had trouble setting the alarm clock in my hotel room that night and it went off later than I wanted the morning of 9/11. I rushed to get ready, knew that I might be late if I waited for the subway, so I hailed a cab. We pulled up after the North Tower was hit. There was a crowd of people just staring and cops started directing traffic away from the scene. The cabbie asked me what I wanted to do and I thought, well the fire looked like it was higher up in the building. Maybe my interview would still go on."

"So I get out of the cab just when I hear this awful sound I'll never forget." Mike's eyes fluttered a bit and Elaina took his hand. "It was the second jet roaring in low right over my head. I ducked, but looked up just as it plowed into the South Tower. There was this huge ball of orange flames and I heard shattering glass, clinking like wind chimes as it fell. People were screaming as bodies started falling. My cab was gone. I freaked out completely, grabbed my suitcase and started running away from downtown as fast as I could. I ran cross country in high school, so it was nothing for me to run a long distance. I ran up Broadway all the way to Central Park. Around West 82nd Street, there was this Catholic church—Holy Trinity—to my right and I ran inside. Figured if I was going to die that day, it would be in a house of God. I found an empty pew in the back of the church and just curled up in a fetal position and cried."

"Oh Josh, how frightening! You must have been exhausted. What did you do after that?"

"A parishioner found me and told the priests. I was in a daze for hours. No one could get me to speak in a complete sentence. She finally managed to get my home phone number out of me and called my family back here in Johnson City to let them know I was OK. I begged the priests to let me stay in the homeless shelter there at the church. I didn't want to travel. Felt so guilty that I lived because of that alarm clock and the guy who was going to interview me must have died. Figured if I stayed put right there by God, I'd be OK. A social worker convinced me finally to go home. Crazy, right? Witnessing all that horror just took away my common sense. My parents drove down and got me a couple of weeks later. It's been a slow road to recovery. I kept telling my therapist, Dr. Kate, about your pie that brought me good luck. That and God, of course. We've been discussing this moment for months. I wanted her to come here with me today, but she said I had to do it alone. These flowers are from our garden at home. Sorry, but that's my mother's good vase, so I'll have to get it back to her eventually."

Elaina took his hands and smiled. "Don't worry about it,

Josh. Listen, this is a big day for you. It's a big day for me, too. You've been returned to me and God couldn't have picked a better time for it to happen. You see, I have this fear I have to stand up to, also. And you've inspired me now. If you could make your way back here, after all the horror you witnessed, I can face the demon in my life. Thank you. This means more to me than you could ever know." She hugged him tightly. They both wept quietly.

"I'm so glad I lived to see you again, Elaina. Sorry to hear you've got your own troubles now. Would it help if you told me what was going on?" She waved her hand away.

"Don't worry about me. I'll be fine. Thanks for asking and thanks for those gorgeous flowers. Listen, you can come up here for free pie any day, OK? Please don't wait until you think the flowers are wilted."

"OK, it's a deal. We'll get through our troubles together."

As soon as he left, Elaina called Rhey.

"Aren't you the bold one, calling a forbidden friend in broad daylight."

"I have fantastic news."

"You left Mitch?"

How did he know? She'd better play dumb. "No, not that great," she laughed.

"Ohhh." Rhey didn't try to hide his disappointment.

"Josh Connelly just stopped in for a visit."

"Who?"

"Remember the kid heading for the interview the day before 9/11? He's alive!" She heard Rhey gasp.

"Are you kidding me? No way!"

"He just wanted to thank me for my kindness that day." Emotion choked Elaina's voice and she couldn't speak. She grabbed a tissue and honked into it.

"Unbelievable."

"Had an awful time on 9/11," she said, her voice shaky. "Witnessed the plane hitting the South Tower. He totally freaked out and was staying in a homeless shelter for a while."

"Poor kid."

"He's been going through therapy. Can't stand airports or the sound of low-flying jets. One landed when he was here and I thought he was going to have a seizure or something. Anyway, his therapist thought it would be a big step if he came up here alone to thank me. I'd joked that day about my pie giving him good luck." She was crying. So was Rhey. He wished this story was about Robbie and that he was found alive somewhere, hiding out on a cruise ship, and that he hadn't contacted him because he was seeing a therapist.

"Rhey, I really need to see a slideshow tonight?"

"Really? Are you kidding? What about...you know?"

"I don't give a damn what he thinks."

"Oooh, I like this new version of you. Get ready world, it's time you met Elaina 2.0."

"Mitch still has my car. Think you could pick me up around seven?"

"Absofreakinlutely!"

"See you then." She hung up and went over to the bouquet to smell the lilies again. After Josh's visit she felt empowered.

She had a suitcase ready to go, the number of an emergency women's shelter and a dear friend ready to help her escape for a fun evening. And Josh was *alive*. What more did she need at that moment? Her destiny was in her hands, it was time to do what she wanted to do with her life.

"I'm getting a ride home, Pop," she said at the end of the workday.

"Here, let me give you some money for the taxi."

"Don't need it. Rhey is picking me up."

"Rhey?" Walt lifted his eyebrow. "What if Mitch...?"

"Mitch can go suck an egg. All right? I'll see you later. Love you, Pop."

What had come over her? She made him laugh, but thoughts of the repercussions that might await her at home concerned him. He hoped she knew what she was doing.

~ Chapter 11 ~

It was readying for a storm.

Stifling heat from the day built up in the gallery and Rhey decided it would be a nice evening to dine al fresco on the patio behind the gallery and watch the slideshow from there when it got dark. He spread a white linen tablecloth over the picnic table, topped it with a metallic gold thread runner and placed a centerpiece of pink cabbage roses in the center. There were gold napkins that matched the runner and he slipped cabbage rose napkins rings around them. Rhey set out gold charger plates, then some lovely floral antique china he'd gotten from Aunt Tillie. The final touch was a pair of crystal wineglasses he'd bought on a shopping excursion in Manhattan with Robbie.

Although Rhey had impeccable design taste, he lacked Elaina's skills in the kitchen. Earlier he drove to the grocery by the mall and bought some brie, baguettes, summer fruit salad, Greek pasta salad and a roasted chicken. Then he stopped to buy some pink champagne at the liquor store. He tooted the horn outside the diner promptly at seven. She came running out, grinning from ear to ear and jumped into his car.

"Buckle up, kids, 'cause Elly's back. Wheeeeee!" Rhey yelled as he floored it out of the parking lot.

"Damn straight!"

When they carried the dinner out to the picnic table and sat down, Rhey opened the champagne first. Elaina held out her champagne glass and he noticed her ring was gone right away.

"Um, El, anything you need to tell me?"

"About what?"

He lifted up her left hand and pointed to her ring finger.

"Explain. *Now.*"

"Let's drink champagne, first."

"Well then, this ought to be good."

There was a light breeze out back as they opened the containers of food. Elaina held her champagne glass up like a chalice, catching the ruby-colored light from the setting sun shimmering on the rising bubbles.

"Do I dare toast to your freedom?" Rhey said as he looked at her hand.

"My eventual freedom, yes." While she was relaxing at the moment, she knew that completely un-tethering herself from Mitch would not be so simple. At that moment, she had no idea if she would return home, stay with Rhey or have him drop her off at the women's shelter for the night. This moment, this wonderful warm summer's eve, she wanted to celebrate life, dine on a menu she hadn't eaten a week ago and not worry that any little move might trigger an angry response.

Rhey was fidgety. He tried eating but wanted to ask her a million questions. Let her eat, let her enjoy the moment, he thought.

"More champagne?"

She looked at her half-filled glass, then at Rhey, and then drained the flute.

"That's my girl."

"I do believe this heat is making me parched," Elaina said in her best Southern accent.

Rhey was happy to comply. The more he poured, the more she might spill about what was going on. He didn't have to wait long to get his wish.

"I'd have worn that beautiful scarf you brought me from Greece, but I couldn't, you see. Mitch is using it to wrap up the pistol he's hiding in his dresser drawer."

Rhey covered his mouth with his hand. The concern he had for his friend and her bad marriage had just changed into a genuine fear for her life—and his.

"El! Did you know he had a gun?"

"Nope. Found it this morning when I was packing up my suitcase to leave. Couldn't find my scarf where I'd placed it. Went looking everywhere for it, through all the closets. Then something told me to check his dresser. I wanted to take the scarf, but I was afraid he'd booby-trapped the drawer and if I pulled on the scarf the gun would go off and kill me."

Rhey reached out to hold her hand.

"Oh, Elly, you must be petrified. Does he know you've run away?"

"Don't know, don't care. He came home very late last night, actually early this morning, drunk, screaming that his damn meat loaf was cold. I was in bed, of course. Too frightened to move. I was afraid he'd beat me up again if I made a noise. Then he phoned someone. Called her 'baby'."

Rhey winced.

"He broke a glass, drank a beer and threw the can down the hall then stormed out. With my car, of course."

"*Wow*! Where's the ring, Elly?"

"I threw it inside the door as I was leaving for work. Maybe he'll crush it when he comes home. That would be symbolic. I'm surprised he didn't stop by the diner today."

"Poor El. You OK with this?"

"Oh, never felt better," she said extending her champagne glass toward him.

"Yes, ma'am, sure 'tis terribly warm this evenin'." Rhey laughed.

They discussed the options before her. Rhey offered to put her up in his apartment as long as she wanted, but she feared it would be the first place Mitch would come looking for her. After much discussion, they agreed that the women's shelter would be her best choice. Then at least she'd still be in town.

"The sheriff's deputy came by last night looking for him; he started questioning me about my relationship with Zahir."

"Hmm," Rhey said, raising his eyebrows. "That's an interesting angle. What did you say?"

"That there's no angle there."

"Yet." Rhey grinned. Elaina slapped his wrist playfully.

"It's getting dark. Bring on the slideshow."

As Rhey stepped back into the gallery, she yelled, "Any more champagne in there?"

"Here you go, El. Now let me see if this new remote

control I ordered for the computer works."

Click, a fabric shop in Barcelona. Click, Aunt Tillie and Rhey eating oysters at a tapas bar. Click, a close-up of a poster for the bullfights. A view of the city from their hotel window. The cruise ship from the dock. The Mediterranean. Click. Click.

Elaina wondered what it must have felt like to see all these images in three dimensions, not as light projected across a field onto a wooden screen. What did the tapas bar smell like? Onions? Garlic? Cumin? Was it windy on the cruise ship? Was it overwhelming to lie back on a chaise lounge on deck and gaze at the starry night at sea? Without the ambient city lights of home, would you see millions and billions of more stars above? Did they make you feel as insignificant as she felt in her marriage?

Her favorite pictures were of Greece, homeland of her mother's family. Had she ever seen sunlight that white-bright, or blue water as mesmerizing as the Aegean? She closed her eyes, swirling the champagne in her glass, as she imagined what a gull's eye view of the Greek Isles would be like. Sirens in the distance distracted her and she frowned, opened her eyes and sighed. "It must have been heaven being on that cruise."

"And then some. Aunt Tillie wasn't stingy with her American Express, either. You need a trip like this, El. Maybe I can get Aunt Tillie to adopt you."

I'd be happy just getting out of Binghamton for a day, she thought.

"Here's the best one," Rhey said as the last picture shone

on the screen. "This is our final sunset on the Mediterranean."

Elaina clasped her hands on the table, and then sighed as she rested her head on them.

"Thank you. I feel like I've been away on vacation."

There was a flash on the screen. For a second, Rhey thought that the projector might have shorted out. The clap of thunder that followed immediately solved that mystery.

"Quick, grab the plates and I'll get the linens. I don't want this tablecloth to get wet."

They raced to carry everything inside as lightning bolts skittered like spider legs across the western sky. Plump raindrops plopped onto the patio as the last of the food was brought through the doorway. There was a very bright flash and then thunder shook the building.

"This one's going to be a doozy. Stay away from the windows, Elly."

Flash! Crash! BOOM!

"I hope we don't lose power," she said as they put the rest of the salads in the refrigerator.

Lightning struck so close it flash-brightened the entire room. They held their breath as they started to count aloud and a crackle-boom followed instantly, followed by rumbling that seemed to last more than a minute. The gallery went dark, but was illuminated immediately by another lightning flash.

"Oh great," Rhey said. "Where did I put those matches?" He felt his way around the kitchen counter.

"I've got the candles here when you find them," Elaina said.

He opened a drawer and rifled through its contents. "Got 'em. Let's get those candles lit."

The candlelight reflected off something on the floor. It was the box of Simon's sculptures.

"Are those for the show?"

"Yes. Still haven't found what I'm looking for, story connection wise. Do you want the ones he gave you to be in the show, too? They wouldn't be for sale, of course."

"Sure. After all, that's how we found out about his talent."

"Remind me, what pieces did he give you?"

"The first was the guy riding the airplane. He left that one on 9/11."

"Spooky."

"The next one was a guy sitting on a skull and crossbones. He left the one of the two guys on the snake right around the time we went to war in Iraq."

"Who are they supposed to be? Bush and Cheney?"

Elaina sat silently. My God, she never thought about it, but that guy with the glasses *did* look like Cheney.

"You're right. Wait a minute. Were these sculptures some type of warning? You've got 9/11, the war in Iraq...but who's the guy on the skull and crossbones?"

"Maybe that's the president again. Didn't we find out around that time that he'd been warned about al-Qaida and Bin Laden planning to attack us?"

"Yeah, you're right. And the last one he gave me was...the guy on the anchor."

They looked at each other at the same time. "MITCH!"

Outside hail pelted the gallery windows. Wind whistled through a partially open window and Rhey jumped up and shut it. Branches from the shrubs scratched at the siding with loud, violent strokes. A strong gust blew open the storm door out front. They ran over to the door together to secure it and another flash of lightning illuminated a car turning into the gallery's driveway.

"Isn't that your car, Elly?"

"*Oh no*, it's him!"

They locked and bolted the gallery door, ran breathlessly into Rhey's apartment and squatted on the kitchen floor by the cabinets. Twirling winds thrashed tree branches against the roof. Thunder rolled like timpani. Another gust lifted fluttered shingles on the gallery's roof.

"Do you think he's out there with the gun?" Rhey whispered.

"Is the back door locked?" she asked, trembling.

"I can't remember. I think so. Weren't you the last to come in when the storm started?"

"Yes, but I don't remember if I locked the door or not."

"We're going to have to check."

They stood up, arms linked, and tiptoed across the hardwood floor. Just as Rhey locked the back door, they heard knocking out front. Elaina screamed but no sound was heard because Rhey's hand clamped down hard over her mouth. Her eyes were wide as they tiptoed back through the doorway that connected his apartment to the inside of the gallery. Flashes of strobe lightning outlined the shadow of a tall man peering into the front gallery window.

Rhey yanked her through the doorway and they skidded onto the kitchen floor.

"Ohmigod, Rhey," Elaina said, teeth chattering. "Did he see us?"

"I don't know. I don't think so. We're safe in here, I think."

Angry, insistent knocking resumed and she gripped Rhey and buried her head in his chest.

"He's not going to get you. I won't let him get you. We're going to be OK. We're going to BE OK! God help us!" They froze when the intruder began twisting the door knob.

A lightning bolt zapped ground nearby followed instantly by a crashing boom. Rain drove at the roof like a thousand nail guns. The volume of the noise made Elaina's ears ring. She thought of Josh and how he reacted when that plane came in low earlier in the day. If Rhey wasn't holding her so tight, she might try running away like Josh did after the terrorist attacks.

They heard a car engine start and saw headlights flash across the gallery's interior then fade away.

"Do you think he's gone?"

"I'll go see," Rhey said. "You stay put." Elaina couldn't stand the thought of waiting there alone and she followed him into the gallery. Rhey peeked out the front window. The only car in the driveway was his. Power returned and the gallery lights turned back on all at once. Elaina shrieked, and then collapsed into sobs.

Rhey went over and hugged her.

"It's OK, it's OK, El. He's gone."

She couldn't stop shaking. The storm calmed and a gentle rain fell outside.

"I thought he was going to come in here and shoot us dead, Rhey. I thought this was our last night on earth. What am I gonna do, Rhey? Do you think Pop is OK?" Rhey didn't want to answer that one.

"Let's call him." Elaina dialed the number and it rang without answer. Why isn't the answering machine kicking in, she thought. Maybe Mitch ripped it out of the wall. "No answer, Rhey. What if he's lying there, dead?"

"I'll drive us over there and see what's going on."

As they headed down Airport Road, they noticed some of the houses had lights on, others didn't. They could see the thunderstorm was now off to the east, flashing over the radio towers atop South Mountain across the river. Rhey had to swerve around tree branches, garbage pails and other debris in the road. Just down the street from Walt's home, flares and fire trucks marked a downed power line. They pulled in Walt's driveway and Elaina ran from the car and knocked. No response.

"Is he there?" Rhey called from the car, looking all around for any signs of Mitch. She took out her old house key and unlocked the door.

"Pop? You here, Pop?"

The living room and kitchen lights were on, but her father wasn't in either room.

"POP! You here?" She ran down the hall to his bedroom. She was afraid to flip the light switch for fear Mitch could be hiding in there. She took a deep breath and flicked it on. Empty. She turned on his closet light. Nothing.

"*Elaina!*" It was her father, calling out from the direction of the living room. She raced back down the hall and found Walt, Rhey and Sgt. Wilcox standing there.

"*Pop!*" Elaina ran to his outstretched arms.

"We just came back from the gallery looking for you."

"Was that you knocking on the door during the storm?"

"No. Listen. You better sit down."

"Why? *WHY*?"

"When did you last see your husband, Elaina?" Sgt. Wilcox asked.

"Yesterday morning. I stayed up late waiting for him to come home but he never did, so I went to bed. Then in the middle of the night, he showed up drunk, angry. He busted a glass and threw the dinner I left for him on the floor. Then he phoned some woman on the phone—he called her 'baby'—and left. I was petrified."

Walt looked at her sympathetically.

"You haven't seen or heard from him since?"

"Well, he may have just paid a visit to the gallery during the storm but we're not sure. Why, what's happened?"

Walt put his arm around her and hugged her.

"I'm afraid I have some bad news," Sgt. Wilcox said. "There was a fire this evening and your apartment burned to the ground. As soon as I heard the report, I drove over there. We didn't know if you had been trapped inside."

Elaina gulped.

"Did it get hit by lightning during the storm? Was Mitch there? *Ohmigod...*did he set it?"

"We're not sure. Too soon to tell. It's a total loss."

She remembered her suitcase of clothes stashed at the diner.

"I left him today. I didn't see him to tell him, but I took off my ring and threw it on the floor before I caught a taxi to work. Maybe he found the ring?"

"We're pretty sure that was him at the gallery tonight," Rhey said. "Right at the height of the storm a car like Elly's pulled up. Some tall man was pounding on the door. We didn't answer it of course. Thank God it started to pour. I think the rain chased him away."

"Do you think it was your car, Elaina?"

She nodded.

"Tell them about the gun," Rhey said.

"Gun?" Walt looked at Sgt. Wilcox.

Elaina spent the next half hour telling the story about the scarf and the earlier occasions when Mitch hit her. Sgt. Wilcox explained how she could press charges against him. He also started asking about Zahir again, which confused her.

"What does he have to do with this?"

"I'm just trying to clarify some details about Mitch's motorcycle crash. We have reason to believe that your husband staged it."

"Oh no. Why would he do that?"

"We found brake fluid dumped on the ground not far from the scene of the crash. It's the same type Zahir uses at his shop.

We think Mitch was trying to frame Zahir."

"That doesn't make any sense. Do you think this is triggered by that post-traumatic stress disorder? Mitch even admitted to me that he thought he had it."

"About that, Elaina. There's something else you should know. We cannot confirm that your husband was ever in the Navy."

"Whaaat?" She fell back into the couch as her jaw dropped. "Ohmigod, he's been lying to me about everything all along. Who is this man I'm married to?"

"Good question. We think it would be a wise idea if you stayed at the Women's Safe Haven for a while instead of home with your father. He'll probably check here or the diner first when he comes looking for you." She nodded to Sgt. Wilcox. "In the meantime, I've put out a bulletin about Mitch and I'll add the info about your car."

"I packed a suitcase this morning and stashed it in the back closet at the diner. Can we go there and pick it up first?"

"Sure," Sgt. Wilcox said. "Ready?" She kissed Rhey and her father goodnight. After they left, Rhey turned to Walt.

"Um, would you mind if I...?"

"You can sleep in Elaina's old room, Rhey. To be honest, I'll sleep better knowing there's another person in the house."

Nothing else happened that night. Nor over the next few weeks. It was right before Labor Day when Sgt. Wilcox visited Elaina in the shelter.

"We found your car. It was abandoned outside of Zephyrhills, Florida. No sign of Mitch. I have a feeling he won't be coming back soon."

"Zephyrhills? So maybe he wasn't lying about his mother living down there."

"Maybe. We spoke with his boss, Mr. Baburka, and he thinks Mitch wasn't alone when he left. I've spoken to the owner of the Glenmere and they confirmed that Mitch was seeing a barmaid there named Kirsten Anderson. Ever met her?"

"No. She was the one who went missing, right?"

"Yes. She's gone again. No one at the Glenmere has seen her since the night of the fire. One friend said she'd told her she was moving out of town. Her family hasn't heard anything from her."

"Do you think it's over? Can I return to work at the diner? Pop must be going crazy."

"Yes, I'd say it's probably safe for now. But you must be extremely careful, Elaina. Stay vigilant. You might never hear from him again or he could show up a couple of weeks, months or even years from now. Until he's caught, you never know what he might do. Here's my card. Carry it with you always."

She grasped the card tightly over her heart.

* * *

It was weird, but that day she felt very lucky. Unlike the other women in the shelter, she could now leave there and wander freely. She'd been given a solution of least resistance to her horrible marriage. The others remained in constant fear for their lives. Mitch, it appeared, left her without looking back. He'd probably already moved on to a new life of lies.

When she returned to the diner, the first pie Elaina baked was pecan—Rhey's favorite. On her break she borrowed Walt's truck and drove to the gallery to surprise him. When she walked in the gallery, Rhey's jaw dropped.

"Is he dead?"

"To me. Not yet to the rest of the world." She held out the pie to him.

"Pecan? My favorite. You're so thoughtful, El." He hugged her and invited Elaina into his kitchen for coffee and pie. "So what happened to him?"

"They found my car in Florida. It appears he fled there with a barmaid from the Glenmere, she was the 'baby' he was cooing to the last night at the apartment. Sgt. Wilcox doesn't think he'll be back. But if any of us see him, he wants us to call him." She took out the card. "Here, write down this number."

Rhey jotted it down on a pad by the phone.

"What's this?" she asked, looking at a sketch on the kitchen counter.

"I'm just finishing the layout for Simon's show. It opens Friday. Guess what? I've finally figured out the story. Now I hope this doesn't freak you out too much, but it looks like every sculpture Simon made is connected to our little universe up here on Mt. Ettrick. See this guy in the little truck. That's gotta be Bill our mail carrier. This waitress in a tornado looks suspiciously like Mary Jo. See the hands of four kids popping out of the funnel? And that kinda looks like a dog on one side and a skunk on the other. I think this other sculpture of a guy holding a wrench is Zahir."

"Wow, that's so cool. Are we in here? Or Pop?"

Rhey held up a man holding a life preserver. "This looks like your father but I don't get the life preserver. And this one I think might be you." He held up a sculpture of a woman on a bridge over a brook with a small bouquet in her hands.

"Wait...can't be...that's impossible." She backed away from the sculpture.

"Huh?"

"You had these sculptures before that happened. This scene was the Sunday when I woke up and Mitch was gone. I went for a walk in the woods by the apartment complex and I discovered this beautiful creek. It was so peaceful there—the calm in the eye of my own hurricane Mitch. This is *it*. That's just what it looked like."

"Are you saying these are psychic sculptures, telling of events to come?"

She nodded to Rhey, wide-eyed.

"Doo-doo-doo-doo," he sang mimicking the "Twilight Zone" theme.

"Man, this is too freaky. So wait a minute. Where's your sculpture?"

He pointed at a figure that looked like the mystery woman Rhey portrayed at the diner.

"Hah! Look, it's the hat you were wearing that day."

"Do you think Mitch is anywhere in this group?" Rhey asked.

"No. He's the guy riding the anchor, of course. I'll have to take a closer look at his face when I get back to the diner. It's weird, all the ones he gave me were warnings and all the ones you got were just future events. Why am I the lucky bearer of catastrophe art?"

"Wait until he shows up at the diner again and ask him."

"Well, on a happier note, Dad thinks it will be OK to go ahead with the party for Dee Dee and Joachim. Will you come as my date?

"Better yet, I'll come as your decorator, too."

"Really? That would be so fun."

"What's her favorite color?"

"Periwinkle."

Rhey winced. "Hmm. That's a tad unfortunate. Transforming the diner's steel and red pleather interior into a vision of tulle and periwinkle may be a challenge, but I do have experience as a miracle worker. Don't I now, Elly?" He held his arms out to her and she nodded, a big grin on her face.

That night when Elaina slept in her old bedroom again, she was revisited by her recurring 9/11 dream. This time she was pulled from the smoke and rubble of the World Trade Center by a man who was wearing a blue shirt, jeans and cowboy boots. She couldn't see his face still, but Elaina wondered if it was Simon. Besides creating psychic sculptures, could he visit her dreams, too?

~ Chapter 12 ~

Freedom *really* isn't free.

Zahir stopped by the next afternoon to pick up a pie he ordered. Angie and Mary Jo were chatting when he came in.

"Here you go, hon," Angie said, handing him the pie.

"Thank you. Did I see Elaina here?"

"Yep. She's out back doing dishes. Wanna talk with her?" He nodded.

When Elaina came out the door, Zahir smiled. She looked rested and her steps were lively.

"Zahir! How are you?" she asked as she rushed over and hugged him. He was startled by her forwardness but was happy to smell that lemony detergent scent again.

"You look very well, Elaina. We missed you here at the diner. I heard you came back home and wanted to come over and say hello."

"Yes. Thank God, Mitch is MIA and I hope he stays there."

Zahir noticed her wedding ring was gone and grinned.

"Sgt. Wilcox said I'm probably safe for now since he ditched our car in Florida, but Mitch might return at any time. We'll all have to stay alert."

"I am always on alert for you, Elaina. Don't worry."

She kissed his cheek and as she backed away, she noticed he was wearing cowboy boots.

"Where did you get *those*? I've never seen you in cowboy boots before."

"It is a funny story. This man's truck broke down a few weeks back. Remember that really bad storm? I was driving past him and pulled over. Helped him out. The battery just needed a charge. He wanted to pay me, and I said no. It was simple to help him; I did no work really. Then he went into the back seat of his car, got out a box and handed it to me. 'Here, thank you,' he said. That's when the wind started to get very bad. I threw the box in the back seat, forgot about it and didn't open it until the next day. Inside were these boots, that fit me perfectly, and a little sculpture made out of aluminum foil."

Elaina's eyes grew wide as she grasped his arm.

"Ohmigod, *tell* me. Was the sculpture a person riding something?"

"No. It was a deer. Why do you ask?" Zahir wondered why there was such a look of relief on her face.

"It's just that I know the guy. That's all. He comes in here occasionally. His name is Simon. Rhey is showing his work at the gallery through September. The opening is Friday night. You should come."

"I will definitely try to make it on Friday, Elaina. We're driving down to Newark to pick up some used cars that day, though. Weird story. That's where we were on 9/11. I was too ashamed and angry to tell you, but we were detained after someone reported seeing us going through the cars in the lot. Malik forgot the paperwork back here at the garage. The owner never showed up because of what was going on at the time. We had no idea about the attacks. Malik was checking to see if keys were in the cars we'd bought from him. The police saw three Saudi Americans acting suspiciously. Couldn't blame them for being careful that day. Charges were soon dropped."

Elaina smiled as she realized her instincts about Zahir were right all along. After he left she walked into the kitchen and took a close look at Simon's sculpture of the man riding the anchor. The man had a cleft in his chin, just like Mitch.

* * *

It was a perfect day for riding back trails in Missoula. Maria and Mort were on their horses, making a slow trek to the ranch in the warm sunshine. Quivering aspens above them were flickering like bright gold candles. The only sounds were hoof-falls of the horses over twigs and leaves. In her mind, Maria wrestled with the decision to leave this refuge of peace and return to Johnson City for the party in honor of her newly married daughters.

"You could just send them wedding gifts," Mort said. "Make up baskets of goods made in Montana. Or mail them a couple of your paintings of the Bitterroots. That might encourage them to come visit *you* instead."

Maria nodded. Why was she so afraid to return home? Did she fear being held captive by her guilt back there? Did she fear never being able to return to her paradise here in Montana? Or was she just afraid to confront the guilt she'd buried within after abandoning her family a decade ago?

"Look," Mort said as he stopped his horse. To their right a mule deer fawn stood frozen in the woods. It was looking straight at Maria, she thought, with the pleading eyes of a child. Its expression reminded her of Elaina and Dee Dee when she first held them. She recalled the warmth of their tiny bodies against her breast, warmth born of her love for Walt. For a second she thought the fawn smiled at her, and then it turned quickly and leapt off into the woods.

"I could take that load back East for the grocery chain. It'd be easy enough to make a detour to Binghamton."

Maria looked up toward the treetops and saw an osprey drifting past, riding a thermal. Her eyes moistened. How could she leave this beauty? Then again, how could she turn her back on her daughters after these important milestones in their lives?

Perhaps it was watching her own mother's life vanish into the routine of the diner that made her flee. Once she emigrated from Greece, Helena never returned. Maria couldn't imagine her mother leaving the beauty of her native land behind forever like that. After Helena married Metro and they moved to Johnson City from their first apartment in Astoria, Queens, Maria's mother never took a vacation, never did anything for herself. All her life was spent taking care of her husband, her daughter and customers at the diner. Maria never recalled seeing Helena read a paperback or go for a stroll. There was always some work related to home or the diner that had to be done. She rarely had any opportunity to relax.

Maria vowed to never live a life as dull her mother's. When Elaina turned sixteen it hit Maria hard: she *was* becoming her mother. Mort just picked an opportune moment to walk into the diner—Maria was desperate for a way out!

"If you do want me to take the load, you'll have to let me know by tomorrow, Maria. Jeff wants me to call him as soon as possible. You decide what is best for you, darlin', and I'll back you one hundred percent."

"Thanks." How could she have been so fortunate, Maria thought, to have such kind gentlemen in her life?

* * *

Mary Jo called in sick Friday. This was a new one. She said she'd had an allergic reaction to hair dye at the beauty salon. She was too distraught to work. Elaina was ticked. She needed to get out early to assist Rhey with Simon's exhibit opening tonight. It didn't look like that was going to happen. The diner was crowded all day. Maybe it was because everyone was getting back to their old routines now that the summer vacation season was over.

Late in the afternoon, she carried out orders for two tables joined together in the back room when she saw Angie waiting on Simon. Drat. She wanted to talk with him about the meaning of his sculptures. The diner was so busy, though, all she could do was wave hello across the room to him.

She didn't feel too bad, though. Hopefully she'd see him at the opening of his show in a couple hours. The customers poured in all day and dinnertime was extremely busy. She ran into the kitchen to slide a couple reserve pies into the oven.

"Pop, I don't know if I'm going to be able to cut out early. It's a madhouse out there."

"Don't worry. Angie and I can handle it. Just leave when

you have to. OK, daughter?"

Elaina arrived at Rhey's gallery a half hour before it opened. She was breathless as she ran through the door, waved at him, and ran into the bathroom to fix herself up. She came out with a new scarf Rhey had given her, tied expertly around her neck.

"Sorry, it got so busy today. Simon came in and all I could do was wave at him. Have you heard from him?"

"No. I hope he's planning to be here. Nice work with the scarf, Grace Kelly." Elaina grinned at Rhey. "Let me do something with your hair," he said. She handed him her brush and he scooped her long tresses into a ponytail then twisted them into a sleek chignon, fastening it with the barrettes she was already wearing. She looked at herself in the mirror and put her hands on her cheeks in surprise.

"How'd you do that so quickly? It's so chic."

"She used the word *chic*," Rhey said folding his hands toward heaven. "Thank you, Lord. My work here is done."

Elaina laughed.

"Just another trick I picked up during my dinner theater days, hah-hah!"

The gallery was full by the time Walt showed up with Angie, laughing as they walked through the door. Rhey noticed the interplay between them and thought maybe something romantic was brewing. After the party, he'd have to remember to ask Elaina if she thought so, too.

"Where's the artist?" Walt asked Elaina, looking around the room.

"He hasn't graced us with his presence yet," Rhey said, leading him over to the figure of the man with the lifesaver.

"Look familiar?"

Walt studied it closely. "Am I supposed to recognize him?"

"Elly and I think it's you."

"Really? Son of a gun. He does have my hair, apron and rugged good looks."

Angie winked at him. "You got that right, hon, and Lord knows you *are* a lifesaver. What would I have done after Mario died if you hadn't hired me?" Oh yes, Rhey thought. Love *is* in the air.

Elaina pointed at another figure. "We think this one is Zahir."

"Were these done by that Indian fella who came into the diner today?" Angie asked as she put her face right up to the mini-Zahir.

"Yes. Did he mention the show?" Elaina asked. "I wanted to talk with him but those two big tables in the back room filled up and I never got the chance."

"I've seen him in the diner before. Kinda odd. Didn't leave no tip. He did leave one of these sculptures on the table and when he paid his bill he said make sure to give it to you. I stuck it on the shelf in the kitchen. You know, where you put the other ones."

Rhey and Elaina looked at each other with alarm.

"What was it? Was there a figure of a man riding something?" Oh God, Elaina thought, I can't use another psychic warning now.

"Nope. It was just a cute little tractor trailer. No one was on it as I recall. But I'd have to take a closer look."

A little while later the door opened and conversation in the gallery ceased. Elaina had her back to the door as she handed a tray of hors d'oeuvres to a waiter to carry around the gallery, but her eyes followed all the heads turned the other way staring at the three Middle Eastern men in the doorway. Rhey heard whispering in the gallery and ignored it.

"Zahir! Welcome!" Rhey made a point of walking over to shake his hand. "I'm delighted to see you made it. Glad you brought some friends, too."

"Hello, Rhey. Nice place you have here. These are my cousins Malik and Arif. They sell the cars, I repair them." Rhey shook their hands.

"Welcome. You know, you should all stop by some Friday night for one of our slideshows. The view's better here than from your home, Zahir."

That made Zahir laugh and the whispering behind them stopped.

Elaina walked toward them. Zahir was wearing those cowboy boots again and a leather jacket over a bright blue shirt and jeans. Boy, he cleans up nice, she thought.

"Hey! I'm so glad you made it. Would you guys like some hors d'oeuvres? Let me get the waiter."

"No thank you. We can't spoil our appetites. My aunt is making dinner tonight for us. Got any spare apple pie we can take over there?" he asked.

"You men and your pie."

"I was just about to show Zahir his sculpture," Rhey said.

"My sculpture? What are you talking about?"

"Take a real close look," Elaina said as he peered at the sculpture. Malik and Arif laughed and pointed.

"It *is* you," Malik laughed. "Look. There's your wrench."

The detail on the sculpture surprised Zahir. The man's hair was parted exactly as his was, and the ears stuck out a little like his own. There was even a stripe across the wrench, just as there was on the large one that hung on the garage wall.

"When did you get this sculpture? Did he do this after I helped him with his car the night of the storm?"

"Oh, no." Rhey said. "I had these before that night. Elly and I have decided that Simon is some sort of psychic sculptor."

"Is that an American Indian tradition?" Arif asked.

Rhey and Elaina shrugged.

"To be honest, we don't know whether to be honored or creeped out by his work," Rhey laughed.

"See this," Elaina said pointing at her sculpture. "I never told anyone about a walk I took one Sunday along the path into the woods behind my apartment. Rhey told me this sculpture was already in the gallery that day. It's exactly what I saw on my walk. That's what really freaked me out."

"I can see why," Zahir nodded. "Look at the detail. Is this really just aluminum foil?"

"That's all—no glue, no staples and no nails," Rhey said. "Simon carves them with toothpicks he gets at Elly's diner."

When the guests had all left, Elaina helped Rhey clean up

the gallery. Six of the sculptures were sold. It wasn't a lot of sales, but Rhey was happy with all the visitors.

"Too bad Simon never made it. I bet we would have sold more of his work," Rhey said as they carried the leftover hors d'oeuvres into his apartment. "Wasn't it nice that Zahir showed up? I think his cousins enjoyed the show," he said taking the plates from Elaina. Rhey grinned when he noticed her blush.

* * *

At that same moment near the Central Gulf Coast of Florida, Mitch sat down across from Kirsten at the kitchen table in a mobile home his mother owned.

"I got you something, baby." He pushed a gift bag toward her and Kirsten grinned.

"Mitch, you've gotta stop spending our money on gifts for me," she winked at him as she parted clumps of tissue paper inside. "Ooh, how pretty," she said as she pulled out a beautiful blue scarf trimmed with sparkly beads. "It looks just like the color of the ocean, sweetie," she said as she draped it over her shoulders and winked saucily at him. Mitch leered at her.

"Hmmm, that's weird, looks like a bead on the end here fell off."

"Oh, that's where the price tag was. Sorry Kirsten, when I ripped it off the big bead came off with it. I threw it in the garbage pail and didn't realize it was missing. Of course, I wrapped this up the day after garbage day, so that big ugly bead is just plain gone."

"Oh well. I guess it isn't needed. The scarf is so beautiful, you wouldn't even notice that a bead was missing."

"So, is dinner ready? If it's Friday, it must be...."

"Fish fry," Kirsten laughed as she clapped her hands together. She was an able cook, but her meals couldn't compare with Elaina's. And forget pies, because Kirsten's crusts were dense and flavorless. She could bake good brownies though.

As Mitch crunched into the crispy fish, he started thinking about how he missed Elaina's pies. He remembered how the crust broke into wafer-thin flakes as your fork cut into it. And he loved how she'd use just Cortland apples, so there'd be a perfect balance of sweet and tart in each bite. Every slice of apple was coated in thick syrup of its own juices mingled with sugar, sweet cream, cinnamon and a hint of nutmeg.

"I got us a key lime pie at the bakery for dessert. They didn't seem to have any apple pies there. That is, if pie is what you really want for dessert," she said leering back at him as she twirled a french fry in her mouth.

Mitch licked his lips as he looked at her lustily. He was trying to decide what he was craving most for dessert: sex or pie? He wasn't going to tell Kirsten, though, that he wasn't even thinking about the key lime pie on the counter. He had a hankering for some *real* pie, and he knew a really good place to get some, up North.

* * *

On Monday morning, plans for the party next weekend were racing through Elaina's mind. She hummed "Here Comes the Bride" as she pulled pumpkin muffins out of the oven.

Whenever she thought of something else that needed to be done, she wrote it down on the to-do list she'd taped to the fridge. After work she was going with Rhey to that craft store on the Vestal Parkway. Tonight they would be seeking ideas for party favors. Pop was also busy planning the food menu. Elaina was going to attempt something she'd never baked: a wedding cake.

While rolling out the pie dough, her thoughts shifted from the party next weekend to the gallery opening Friday night. She recalled how handsome Zahir looked when he walked in. Man, she'd never noticed the breadth of his shoulders before, as they were set off smartly by his tailored leather jacket. That blue shirt brought out the color of his eyes intensely and she never noticed his long delicate fingers that belied his chosen profession. I wonder if he's at work yet, she thought as she went into the dining room and peeked out the front window. Zahir had just rolled up the garage door and was looking right toward her.

Elaina wondered, can he see me? She waved. He smiled and waved back. Ohmigod, he *can* see me. She pretended to check the salt and pepper shakers, to make him think that was her true purpose for being in the dining room at that moment, and then scurried back into the kitchen laughing to herself.

Dee Dee called later that day and spoke with Walt. She told him they would arrive Friday afternoon and go right to his house.

"Drive safely, Dee Dee," Walt said as he handed the receiver to Elaina.

"Hey, Dee Dee! What's up?"

"Hey, Sis. Just checking in with Pop. Ready to party Saturday?"

"Absolutely! Rhey and I are having so much fun planning all the details for your *soiree.*"

"Oh, so now it's a *soiree,*" Dee Dee laughed. "You must be so happy, Elaina, now that you're free of that jerk." There was an awkward pause.

"Yeah, I'm pretty happy the old ball and chain isn't around anymore."

"Has anybody heard from him?"

"Nope, and I hope no one does. I'm just not going to think about him; especially this weekend with all the relatives here. Can't wait for the Brady bunch reunion."

Dee Dee thought that was an optimistic wish. How could Elaina truly put him out of her mind and not always worry if he'd return?

"Well, Sis. Joachim and I will be there Friday about three o'clock."

"Great! See you soon."

* * *

Elaina had the dream again that night. It started with the man wearing cowboy boots reaching out to grab her hand and pull her from the burning tower. This time she was determined to find out who he was.

"Zahir? *Zahir?* Is that you?"

There was no answer. The thick smoke obscured the man's face. Before she knew it, she was outside once again in the sunshine, breathing fresh air.

"No!" she yelled as she headed back into the inferno. "Tell me. *Please*. Who are you?"

Stand back and you won't get hurt, she heard in her mind. It wasn't the man's voice; it was his thoughts speaking to her.

Elaina sat up in bed with her heart pounding. She was sweating and wiped her brow with the back of her hand. Who *is* this person? If it's not Zahir, is it Simon? After all, he gave the cowboy boots to Zahir. When are these dreams going to end? Would she ever find out who this guy is?

* * *

Wednesday morning Mort pulled the tractor trailer into a rest stop to fuel up for their trip.

"Want anything, Maria?"

She smiled. "No thanks, I'm fine." Was she? Had she made the right decision? As soon as they pulled out of Missoula a feeling of dread began to grow in the back of her mind. Why? They were heading back East for a celebration, so what was this ominous feeling about? Was she was nervous and afraid of the response they'd encounter back in Binghamton? Mingled with that fear was a spark of joy. She'd be seeing her daughters again in a few days. Maria wondered if the girls would look more like her or Walt.

Mort came out of the convenience store carrying two cups of coffee and a bag of doughnuts.

"Thought you might want this anyway," he said as he handed the bag and a cup to her. She laughed to herself. He knows me too well.

"Do you think I'm doing the right thing, Mort?"

"Well, we're getting paid for this trip, so that's good. Nothing to lose. You know what darlin'? I'm really looking forward to meeting your girls and Walt, though he might not feel the same way about me. He sounds like a good man."

"He is. Too good for me," she said. Just like you Mort, she thought.

"Now none of that negative talk, Maria." He kissed her cheek. "Let's enjoy this adventure together and pray your ex-husband doesn't 'welcome' me with a rifle."

* * *

You'd have thought Rhey was staging a Broadway show. He kept stopping by the diner all week to show Elaina choices for linens and flower arrangements and, of course, napkin rings. He'd sketch out his ideas and drive over with them so they could discuss everything during her break at the picnic table.

"Here's where we'll place the dais for the wedding party," he said on Thursday as he pointed at a map of the diner's L-shaped interior. "I'll set up some potted trees in groupings here, here and over there. My friend Richie works at the florist supply warehouse and can give me a great deal on the rentals. The cake will sit on a table right here in the corner, so guests sitting on both sides of the dining area can see them cut it. Have you figured out what the cake will be like yet?"

Elaina pulled out a piece of paper from her apron pocket and showed Rhey a sketch of the wedding cake.

"Did you draw this?" She nodded. "I didn't know you

could draw this well. This is beautiful."

"Well, I've been inspired by the stuff I've seen in your gallery. I bought a real sketch pad at the craft store last week and have been doodling in it every day."

"Elly, you have genuine talent. *Wow.* We'll have to develop this new skill of yours."

Rhey said she had a talent, besides making pies. Elaina felt so happy.

Walt called from the door to them. "Your sister's on the phone." She ran inside.

"Hey, Elaina, how are the plans for the party going?"

"Great, Dee Dee. Rhey was just showing me his design. It's going to be so beautiful inside the diner. He really is an *artiste.*"

Dee Dee laughed. Thanks to Rhey, Elaina was getting a whole new vocabulary.

"By the way, Sis, there's something I have to tell you." The serious tone of Dee Dee's voice frightened Elaina. Oh no, had Mitch contacted her?

"I've been debating whether or not to tell you this when I got there or do it now. I don't want you to be angry, so I figured it'd be best to tell you before I arrive. You must promise, and I mean it, not to say anything to Pop."

Elaina leaned against the wall by the phone to brace herself for the news. Did Dee Dee have cancer? Was she pregnant and something is wrong with the baby? Are they having trouble with their marriage? Was Joachim's visa revoked somehow? Thoughts streamed through her mind rapidly like information beaming to earth from a satellite.

"I called Mom and asked her to come to the party."

"You *WHAT?*" Elaina felt like the air was punched out of her. "Why? What the hell made you do that? Why should *she* be here?"

"Don't be angry. Please. I just thought she might want to be here for our celebration. She is our mother, after all."

Elaina was stunned. How could Dee Dee do something so stupid? This was going to freak their father out. Why do that to him on a day when their family could celebrate some happiness finally?

"Sis? Are you there? Do you hate me?"

Elaina turned toward the front door so Walt couldn't hear her. "No...just confused. Don't understand why you would think she'd even come. How did you find Mom?"

"It was actually not that difficult. I googled her name and this newspaper story came up from Missoula. She was in a photograph posing with her horse next to a man. The caption said his name is Mort Beoman. I looked up Mort's name in an online phone directory, called the number and Mom answered."

"What did she say? Was she surprised?"

"Shocked pretty much describes her reaction. She asked about you. I told you were married. It was before Mitch disappeared, so she thinks this party is to celebrate both of our marriages."

"Is she coming?"

"She said she'd think about it. My gut tells me she will be

here. She sounded so nice, Elaina."

"Man, how's Pop gonna feel on his big day when Mort walks in? He'll think we're traitors, that we don't love him anymore. This can only be a disaster, Dee Dee."

"I don't know. God, I hope not. Man, what was I thinking," Dee Dee paused. "It wouldn't be like Pop to be ungracious to Mort, though. Who knows? They might get along swell."

Elaina looked over her shoulder at her father flipping a cheeseburger on the griddle.

"I wonder what she'll think of us all now. I've missed her, Elaina. Haven't you?"

"I really have, Dee Dee. Maybe she won't show and we'll be worrying for nothing. I'm kinda glad one of us finally spoke with her, though. I wonder what Mort's like."

"Well, from the photo in the paper I can tell you that he's good looking, in a hunky cowboy kinda way."

"Hmm.... Well, this should be real interesting. Thanks for the warning, Sis. See you Friday."

When Dee Dee mentioned the word truck, Elaina remembered that she hadn't taken a close look at that latest sculpture Simon left behind. She wondered if there was a connection. Elaina walked into the kitchen and picked up the tractor trailer. Inside the cab were a man and a woman. Was that her mother and Mort inside? Did this mean something bad might occur? Then she thought about the other sculptures he had left her. They all involved someone riding on something. Maria and Mort were riding *in* the truck. Did that mean a reversal of fortune? Did that mean this signified something good was about to happen?

Elaina walked back into the dining room when an older couple came in. As the man held the door open for his wife, a cold gust of wind blew in across Elaina's face. She pulled her cardigan closer and shivered as she let the thoughts of future possible danger flash through her mind like one of Rhey's picture shows.

* * *

Nervous tension rose in Maria that afternoon as they crossed into the Midwest. Her palms were sweaty and she became hyper-aware of her breathing. For a moment, she felt faint and dizzy. Was she having a panic attack or was something else going on with her? Her mother had heart trouble at her age. Did she inherit the same weakness? Maria debated whether she should tell Mort or just hold on quietly and see if the symptoms pass. He had already noticed that she looked pale, as if the residual sunshine from her life outdoors was fading the farther east they got.

They stopped to refuel in Minneapolis and Mort walked around the trailer to inspect it. The back right tires felt like they were dragging back there on the highway, but they looked all right up close. He checked the tire pressure and it was where it should be. Maybe when they got to Johnson City he'd have a mechanic take a look at them. Mort prayed that the tires would just hold on so they could make it in time for the Bradys' party. This was an emotional moment for Maria, and he didn't want to add to her stress.

~ Chapter 13 ~

The familiar beckoned.

When Mitch opened the door to the trailer Thursday evening, he expected to smell his favorite meal being cooked. There was no aroma of freedom fries baking in the oven. Kirsten wasn't standing over the stove, stirring chipped beef into the white sauce.

"Where's my dinner, baby?"

"You know, babe. I gotta be honest with you," she said as she walked in the room all dressed up. "I'm tired of chipped beef Thursday. We need a little change to spice up our life. I don't know anyone here yet. I'm so bored all day while you're out working at the golf course. I really need you to take me out to dinner. Look, I wore your favorite dress," she purred.

Mitch's hands hung at his sides, clenching into fists and releasing.

"You need a change. Is that so? That's a shame 'cause you know Thursday's menu is my favorite one of the week."

"Oh, and I checked again. I don't think that bakery ever sells apple pie. They had key lime and coconut cream and chocolate cream, but no apple. I walked across town to the grocery and found a frozen apple pie, so I baked it for you. I figured we could come back here for dessert, if you know what I mean."

Mitch stared at the baked frozen pie on the counter. Instead of having a plump center like Elaina's pies, this one went straight across like a flat-lining EKG. He pulled open the refrigerator door with a force that startled Kirsten, grabbed a beer, popped the lid and took a big swig. He walked over to the sink, stared out the window and squeezed the can so hard the beer flowed over into the sink.

"Sure. Baby says she wants to go out, so we're going to go out for dinner. There's a new place across the highway from the pond. We can walk there instead of taking the bus. It's a cool evening. Let me go change my shirt, honey baby. Why don't you wait for me outside?"

Mitch went into the bedroom, pulled a duffle bag off the closet shelf and stuffed it with a week's worth of clothing, including the Navy uniforms he'd stolen from that girl in Syracuse's father. His pistol was stashed behind the pipes under the bathroom sink cupboard. The bullets were rolled into some tube socks in his dresser. He loaded the gun, tucked it in his pants and buttoned up his long Hawaiian shirt over it.

"I can't wait until we have enough saved for a new car." Kirsten said as they started down the road out of the mobile home park. "It was too bad ours broke down so bad we had to abandon it."

"That *was* too bad."

* * *

After he'd rolled Kirsten's body into that swamp near the pond, Mitch washed the blood off his arms and walked back to the trailer calmly where he changed into the white Navy uniform and hitched a ride north on the highway. The tractor trailer of the driver who stopped to pick him up had American flag decals on either side of his cab that read "These colors don't run."

The driver nodded when Mitch climbed into the cab.

"Where are you heading, sailor?"

"Upstate New York. Been visiting family down here and heading back home to the wife."

"Have you been over there in the war?"

"Yes sir. I got back from my deployment a couple months ago. I expect I might be called up again soon."

"Where were you? Persian Gulf?"

"Can't disclose that, sir. Special Ops."

The trucker smiled. "I'm honored to give a young patriot like you a ride then."

* * *

Deputy Draper was at the main desk Saturday morning when the interstate bulletin came in about a woman found shot dead Friday. Her body was floating in a swamp outside of Zephyrhills, Florida. She had no identification on her and the Florida police sent out the bulletin in case she matched the description of a missing woman anywhere.

He shook his head. It was a story he'd heard too many times in his career. Another pretty young woman found dead. How could promising lives meet such terrible ends?

When the photo accompanying the fax came through, he looked at it and his stomach churned seeing the trauma she'd suffered. Something compelled him to take a closer look, difficult as it was. There was something familiar about this woman.

* * *

When Mort and Maria reached Buffalo on Saturday afternoon, he was ready to get a room and give Maria a chance to get a good night's sleep to prepare for the big event. Her eyes had a look of urgency, though, to press onward. She was so close now to her old home; the pull of seeing her daughters was too strong. In less than four hours they could be there.

He refueled at a rest stop and bought some ham sandwiches and coffee for them. Maria went into the restroom to splash water on her face and brush her hair. She was surprised that her previous trepidation was giving way to unbridled joy. In a few hours she'd be hugging her daughters. She couldn't wait. Maria missed them more than she let on to Mort. Wow, they were both already married. Maria wondered what their reactions to her would be. The last morning she'd seen them, she'd braided their hair. Tonight she'd be shaking hands with their husbands. Yes. This was absolutely the right decision.

* * *

Rhey drove up to the diner and carried in a box of decorating supplies.

"Perfect timing," Elaina said holding the door. "Last customer just left."

Walt hung up his apron as they unloaded yards of tulle and strands of tiny white lights.

"Well this ought to be something," he laughed as he stood

there, hands on hips, watching them work. "Can't wait to see what you'll do to the place."

"Expect nothing short of Camelot," Rhey laughed as he draped the tulle around his arms like a feather boa. "Now run along, Walt. Elly and I have magic to work."

"Will do. Dee Dee and Joachim are taking me out for spiedies. Nice to get a night out. Oh, by the way, I told Zahir to bring his cousins tomorrow, too. So we might need two more place settings."

"Got it, Pop. See you later."

Elaina's heart leapt as she glanced over at the garage and saw the light was still on.

"Need I remind you, Miss Elly," Rhey brushed her arm with the tulle, "that you're still married? You can't be having any lustful thoughts until you're free."

She lowered her eyebrows at him.

"OK, Debbie Downer." They laughed.

Rhey brought the ladder into the dining room so they could take down the curtains and drape the tulle across the windows like bunting. Elaina was twisting the lights into the tulle and holding it up to Rhey. Once they got that hung, Rhey was ready to fasten the silk hydrangea blossoms at the points where the fabric looped around the curtain rod.

"Hand me the glue gun Elly," he said. She looked on the counter but it wasn't there. She checked the box, it wasn't there either.

"Where'd you put it, Rhey?"

"It should be in the box."

"Not there. I checked already."

"Oh for the love of Elvis, did I leave it back at the gallery?" he said as he climbed down the ladder. He poked through the bags of decorations on the counter.

"I'll dash back home and get it. You can fold the napkins into fans while you're waiting. Let me show you how it's done."

* * *

After catching a ride from a Canadian trucker in Harrisburg, Mitch was fortunate to be driven all the way to Binghamton. The driver stopped at a diner on Front Street and Mitch got out and called a cab. "I need a lift to the airport," he told the dispatch person.

As the cab neared the top of Mt. Ettrick, Mitch saw a farmhouse with its lights on down the bend from the diner.

"Hey, I see my friends are home. Stop at this house. They'll give me a lift to the airport from here."

Mitch paid the cabbie and strode up the long driveway. As soon as the taxi cab turned around and headed down the hill out of sight, he walked back to the road, crossed it and headed up toward the diner.

* * *

Maria was so excited she was biting her fingernails. As they passed homes with their lights on, she wondered what her old home looked like now. What would Walt's reaction be when he saw their trailer pull up in the diner's lot? She wondered if Elaina was working there now, too. Would their arrival be met with happiness or awkwardness? Hopefully Dee Dee would be there to smooth over the surprise.

Mort took the exit off the highway and he thought he felt dragging back on the right side of the trailer. He was definitely going to have a mechanic look at those wheels before he left town for the delivery to the grocery warehouse in Boston. When he turned left at the bottom of the ramp off Route 17 East onto Airport Road, the load shifted a bit and he felt it again. Something was definitely wrong on the right side of the trailer.

* * *

Mitch walked stealthily toward the diner. This time he'd *really* get even with her for leaving him. Where did Elaina get the idea that she was better than him? He'd love to make her swallow that ring she threw on the floor. *Bitch!*

He thought it would be better to leave his duffle bag down the road, out of sight, in case he had to make a getaway. He'd run down here, grab it and dash back into the woods. Just ahead there was a small produce stand next to a display of pumpkins. He stashed the duffle bag behind it.

* * *

Simon was driving his horse back from the farm in Glen Aubrey where the Chinese woman did acupuncture on injured animals. He turned off Knapp Road onto Airport Road and when he passed the diner, he slowed. There was Elaina dancing by herself with tulle wrapped around her arms. As she danced happily in a circle with her arms outstretched, it reminded him of the dance the people of his nation did to drive away evil spirits. Simon nodded as he drove on. Something made him look back in the rear view mirror to glimpse at her dance once more. That's when he saw the man dressed in white walk out of the darkness onto the shoulder of the road below the diner's parking lot. Simon knew it was danger approaching. He began to chant as he closed his eyes tightly and morphed Elaina's dancing image in his mind into a leaping white-tailed deer.

* * *

"We're almost there, Mort! I'm so excited." Maria was leaning forward in her seat to get the first glimpse possible of the diner. Mort sensed her excitement and sped up. Just as they rounded the bend near the diner, Maria saw a flash of white in the headlights and screamed.

"Look out! *Deer!*"

Mort slammed the brakes and one of the back right tires flew off. The trailer did a 360 spin to the left as the diner loomed ahead.

Rhey was driving back to the diner when he saw the tractor trailer out of control. He pulled off the road and watched in slow-motion horror as the back of the trailer aimed right for the diner windows.

Zahir had just locked the garage when he saw the tire go airborne, the tractor trailer spin then tip onto its side and the cab scrape the road.

Elaina heard brakes squeal, metal scrape pavement, gravel pinging the diner's front window and popping explosions as the neon sign toppled. She froze in shock, looking out at the end of the trailer which now sat a couple of feet away from the window where they'd just draped the tulle.

She snapped out of her stupor, grabbed the phone and dialed 911. Zahir had already climbed on top of the cab and was talking to the people trapped inside. He ran back to the garage to get some tools and pried off the door. Rhey ran up breathlessly around the far side of the overturned truck and headed toward the diner's front door. "Elly! *Elly!* Are you OK?" She ran outside the diner to him and they hugged. Then they ran over to help Zahir.

"Are they alive in there? Are they injured?"

"I think they're OK. Did you call 911?"

"Yes." Approaching sirens whined in the distance. Soon the police and an ambulance arrived. They set up flares and blocked traffic.

Zahir continued talking with the people inside the cab calmly until the EMTs rushed to the scene so they could examine the trapped couple. Elaina put her hands on her head as she walked over to get a look at the diner's neon sign, crumpled like aluminum foil. Man, she thought, why did this have to happen right before Dee Dee's party?

The EMTs lifted the woman out of the cab and put her on a stretcher. She was pointing at the restaurant as one of them spoke with her. The woman was agitated and Elaina could hear her voice where she was standing.

"You don't understand. This used to be my diner. I used to work here. I'm Maria Brady."

Elaina's jaw dropped. "*Mom?* Is that you?" She ran to her mother's side. "Mom! It's me, Elaina!"

"Oh...*Elaina!*" They hugged tightly. "This is Elaina, this is

- 235 -

my eldest," she told the EMT.

"What happened, Mom?"

"Well, we came around the bend and this deer came out of your parking lot down the road. It didn't dart across our path; the deer leapt straight at us. It was odd."

The EMTs pulled Mort carefully out of the cab. His wrist appeared injured, the way he was holding it, and he had a gash above his right eye but it didn't look too serious.

"We must have lost a back wheel when I braked," Mort told a sheriff's deputy, "the way we tipped over so fast. It's a miracle we're not injured more. Can't say the same for that deer, probably."

"He's right," another deputy said. "A back right wheel is missing. Wonder where it ended up?" he took a flashlight and looked on the shoulder down below the diner. He saw skid marks where the exposed metal cut into the pavement, but there was no wheel. When he flashed the light toward the sign, he saw a bit of white sticking up.

"Looks like your deer might be down there."

The back door of the trailer had sprung open on impact and frozen food spilled all over the parking lot and lawn next to it. As the deputy got nearer, he realized that it wasn't a deer lying there in the grass next to giant letters spelling The Terminal Diner. It was a pant leg. He pushed back the boxes of frozen Montana huckleberry pies and saw a body of a man, knocked dead by the giant tire next to him. The deputy signaled to the EMTs, and soon a group gathered around the dead man.

"What's going on over there?" Maria asked.

"That guy said something about a deer. I'll go check. Rhey, you stay with my mom."

As Elaina walked around the truck toward the diner, she thought of the sculpture Simon left of the tractor trailer. This was what it was warning us about, she thought. Instead of heading straight over to the circle of men, something made her run into the diner to take another look at Simon's sculpture. She picked it up and the back right wheel fell off. Her hands shook as she tried to reattach it and that's when she noticed the anchor pressed into the underside.

Mitch. *Mitch!* That's no deer out there she thought. She raced back outside toward the people gathered there.

"Ma'am, I don't think you want to come any closer. It looks like we've got a fatality here."

"No, I have to. I think I know who it is."

She pushed past the crowd just as an EMT was lifting off the pies to get a better look.

"Be careful, son," the deputy said. "There's a pistol lying right there by his hand."

"Ohmigod, it's him! *Mitch!*" she screamed, and her whole body began to shake. "He was coming to kill me!" She backed away from his dead body, as if she expected her husband to spring to life.

And then a hand took hers from behind and the blue sleeved arm curled around her, folding her into an embrace.

"You're safe now, Elaina. You won't have to live in fear any more. Never again."

In the light from the diner, Zahir's eyes looked even bluer in that moment than the day he helped her after her car slid into the ditch. She held her angel tightly and didn't let go.

* * *

The police investigated the accident and determined that Mort was not at fault for the death of Mitch. However, he was fined for driving the load with faulty back right wheels.

Mort sprained his left wrist when the cab tipped over and Maria suffered a broken rib. After he got over the initial shock of his wife's return, Walt invited them to stay with him until they healed well enough to drive back to Montana. Zahir was making good progress on repairing the rig, too.

They had a small celebration for Dee Dee and Joachim a few weeks later. Walt had secretly arranged with Father Dwyer, Dee Dee and Joachim to have a church wedding. It was just immediate family plus Joachim's sister who was visiting from Germany, Rhey, Zahir and Angie. Mary Jo's son had a soccer tournament out of town so she couldn't make it. Rhey set up a tent behind his gallery for a catered dinner. He didn't want anyone cooking, though Elaina made the wedding cake.

It was a warm fall afternoon, and when evening fell, hundreds of tiny white lights illuminated the ceiling of the tent. It reminded Elaina of what she imagined the night sky viewed from a cruise ship looked like.

Conversations around the table were lively. Maria watched the dynamics between Walt and Angie. It made her happy to see a relationship about to bloom into love.

"You have such a beautiful smile," Maria said to her.

"Yes she does," Walt said with a big grin as he patted Angie's hand. She tilted her head and gave him a funny look.

"Walter Brady! Was it *you* who paid my bill?"

He winked and sipped his glass of Irish whiskey. Angie planted a big kiss on him and everyone in the tent roared with approval.

Maria's gut feeling was right about how Walt and Mort would get along. If you just met them tonight, you'd think they were old high school buddies, she thought. The girls made Mort feel right at home, too. She was proud of her ex-husband for the great job he did raising them alone.

"DJ" Zahir was playing some Arabic techno and everyone got up to dance. Walt, who hated dancing, used the moment to pull Maria aside and go for a walk around the building.

"So you'll be leaving soon, Maria?"

"Yes. My pain is subsiding and Mort's wrist is manageable now. If he gets tired driving back, I'll help out."

"You? Driving an eighteen-wheeler?" Walt laughed.

"Pie makers can do anything, Walt. We're a super breed."

He paused and took her hands. "We had some great times together, didn't we, Maria?"

She grinned. "Remember the night at the stadium?"

He smiled widely, sighed and then looked at the ground. "Could I just ask you one question, Maria?"

She had the answer ready before he ever asked it.

"It had absolutely nothing to do with you as a person, Walt. I saw how this diner robbed my mother of her own life and I just wanted more. I know, it sounds so selfish. You never did a thing wrong. And if you're wondering why Mort, it's because he reminded me so much of you, back under the stadium seats that night. He was a version of you, but free of the weight of that damn diner."

Her words didn't wipe away his years of pain, but he was glad he got to hear her reasons and was relieved that it wasn't him. Mort *was* a good man. If she couldn't be with him, at least she'd found a man who would take good care of her. They hugged and Walt felt the weight of years of sadness and anger slide off his back.

Maria cherished the time she got to spend with her girls there, too. Dee Dee had definitely inherited her temperament and Elaina, Walt's. She could sense that Joachim was the perfect match for Dee Dee, too. Zahir was a fine young man and if his relationship with Elaina became more serious, he had Maria's approval.

Although Mort had no control over the accidental death of Mitch, Maria felt it was a bit of karmic justice at work. She was happy to free Elaina from her hellish marriage and was glad to be the vehicle, literally, for her deliverance. Who knows what possibilities her daughter's life now had?

Before they headed back to Montana, Mort and Maria stopped at the diner for one last cup of coffee with pie. "Wow, Yia Yia Helena would be proud of you, Elaina," Maria said as she ate a slice of apple. "You've mastered her crust technique."

"Well, I had a great teacher," Elaina said.

"You still have." Maria smiled as they embraced.

Walt and Mort were talking with Zahir as Maria and

Elaina walked out to the cab to say farewell.

"Promise you'll come out and visit us in Montana. Tell that father of yours to give you at least a two-week vacation, too."

Walt came over to help Maria into the cab and heard the end of the conversation. "Shouldn't be a problem, Elaina, we'll have Mary Jo fill in for you. She's racked up enough 'I-owe-you-one' points for you to have a nice long trip out West."

"Thanks, Pop," Elaina said taking his arm.

"Don't forget to bring Zahir to visit us, too," Maria smiled, pointing behind Elaina. Zahir walked over and took Elaina's hand.

"Yes, but I'll come only if you promise to show me how to ride the bucking bronco."

* * *

The day the new neon sign was being installed, Sgt. Wilcox stopped by to speak with Walt and Elaina. Rhey was having coffee at the counter and listened in to their conversation.

"His name was Jay Mitchell. He was from Salamanca, out near Buffalo. His parents were divorced—he told you the truth about that at least. His mother lives in Zephyrhills but was visiting relatives in New Jersey when Mitch, I mean Jay, moved into her mobile home. His father lives in Horseheads where he sold fake IDs, passports and is under investigation for trafficking kiddie porn."

Rhey's eyes widened and he mouthed to Elaina "I told you so." She closed her eyes and chuckled to herself then put her finger to her mouth and shook her head at him.

"We believe he stole the Navy uniforms from the father of

a girl he was dating in Syracuse, Ned Johnson. Ned's daughter Tina and Jay hadn't been heard from since the Saturday right before 9/11. His former girlfriend in Salamanca, an American Indian girl named Sharon Seneca, went missing the previous May. They found her skeletal remains in the Chemung River."

Elaina shuddered as Walt put his arm around her and drew her close to him.

"What was his connection to the Binghamton area?"

"We're not sure. It's easy for people to drift through here with so many interstates connecting. Perhaps there is another victim here. You were the only woman he appears to have married."

"Ugh. Lucky me."

Outside a crane hoisted the diner's new neon sign in place. They all gathered to watch.

"'Walt's Place.' I like the sound of that. Catchy name," Sgt. Wilcox winked as he shook his hand.

"You take care now, Elaina." He tipped his hat toward her.

"Thank you very much for all you and the department have done."

"My pleasure."

Elaina carried the hot water pot over to the last booth and refilled the empty mug.

"Anything else I can get you today, Simon? How 'bout a slice of apple crumb pie just out of the oven?"

As he dunked a tea sachet in the mug. Simon looked out the window at the new neon sign and nodded.

"Men *do* like pie."

9163205R0

Made in the USA
Charleston, SC
16 August 2011